HAT TRICK

Also by Jacqueline Guest
in the Lorimer Sports Stories series:

HAT TRICK

Jacqueline Guest

James Lorimer & Company Ltd., Publishers
Toronto

James Lorimer & Company Ltd., Publishers acknowledges the support of the
Ontario Arts Council. We acknowledge the financial support of the Government
of Canada through the Canada Book Fund for our publishing activities. We
acknowledge the support of the Canada Council for the Arts for our publishing
program. We acknowledge the Government of Ontario through the Ontario
Media Development Corporation's Ontario Book Initiative.

Library and Archives Canada Cataloguing in Publication

Hat trick / by Jacqueline Guest.

(Sports stories)
Issued also in an electronic format.
ISBN 978-1-55277-563-9

I. Title. II. Series: Sports stories (Toronto, Ont.)

PS8563.U365H37 2010   jC813'.54   C2010-903309-4

James Lorimer & Company Ltd.,
Publishers
317 Adelaide Street West, Suite 1002
Toronto, ON, Canada
M5V 1P9
www.lorimer.ca

Distributed in the United States by:
Orca Book Publishers
P.O. Box 468
Custer, WA USA
98240-0468

Printed and bound in Canada
Manufactured by Friesens Corporation in Altona, Manitoba, Canada in August 2010.
Job # 58197

CONTENTS

For Mary with love—thanks for the years of patience, understanding and positive pressure—and for my husband Gordon, who had faith.

1 BAD CALL

Leigh Aberdeen tightened her grip on her hockey stick. Her eyes flicked to the player on her left. His gaze was riveted on the ref's hand, which held the puck.

The puck hit the ice and Leigh's reflexes took over. She cut in front of the other player, outmanoeuvred him and headed down the ice. She watched as the centre for her team sent the puck speeding out to meet her. Swerving, Leigh intercepted the puck and turned toward the far net. She could hear the crowd screaming.

Her team, the Forest Park Falcons, were tied with the Devon Dynamos with two minutes left in the third period. This was the closest they'd come to beating their arch rivals all season.

Leigh caught a glimpse of both Dynamo defence-men streaking toward her. If she could keep out of their reach, she had a good chance of setting up her shot well enough to beat the Dynamo goalie.

Suddenly, out of the corner of her eye, she saw the flash of a green uniform. It was Jimmy Crane, the captain of the Falcons, coming up on her side, fast. What was he doing? He should be running interference for her with the two Devon players.

"Pass me the puck," Jimmy shouted at her.

"I'm nearly set up!" she yelled back through her face mask. "Take these two out." She dodged around one of the defencemen who'd caught up with her.

"I'm the captain. I call the plays," Jimmy said, bumping her out of the way.

Leigh was so surprised, her stick jerked, sending the puck spinning out of control down the ice.

Her balance was way off. She felt her skates starting to slip. Her arms automatically came up to help centre herself. Unfortunately, when her arms came up, so did her stick. She felt the butt end hit the shoulder of the Dynamo defenceman who had moved in behind her.

The whistle went before she had a chance to lower her arms. The ref was pointing at her and signalling with his hands. Leigh knew she had a two-minute penalty for high-sticking.

There was only time for one more play, and now the Falcons would be shorthanded. She sat in the penalty box, watching as the two teams formed up for a faceoff in Falcon territory.

The puck hit the ice with a smack. Both centres were on it instantly. The Falcon centre tapped it out to a defenceman who passed it up ice to the waiting forward. Leigh held her breath. If he could make a break for it, he might get a chance to score. The Dynamos were all over the guy. He had no one to pass to until the other defenceman could break out. The Falcons needed their extra forward, the one sitting in the penalty box.

Leigh watched as the two Devon defencemen moved in on the lone Falcon forward. They stripped him of the puck, turned and headed back toward the Falcon goal.

It was amazing to see what a difference one extra player on the ice could make. The Dynamos headed down the ice like a killer wave. The Falcons tried to intercept the passing, but they were spread too thin. Leigh watched as the Dynamos passed the puck back and forth, waiting for their chance.

The puck went rink wide as one of the Dynamo forwards passed it to his partner. Suddenly, the Dynamo centre cut to the slot area just as the far winger passed the puck into him. He turned, and slammed the puck into the far corner of the Falcon goal.

The Dynamo fans went wild. The horn sounded, ending the game. Dynamos 3, Falcons 2.

Leigh looked across at her team's bench, but no one even glanced her way. After a quick handshake for the winning team, the Falcon players grabbed their equipment and headed for the dressing room.

Leigh didn't need to be there to know what the guys were saying. As the only girl on the team, she changed in the women's washroom, and right this minute, she was glad she didn't have to face her teammates.

Leigh sighed. Letting your whole team down by pulling a stupid penalty and losing the game was a poor start to the NHL career she dreamed of. She wondered if Manon Rhéaume had ever messed up and cost her team the game.

She took off her shoulder pads and threw them at her equipment bag. She hadn't meant to high-stick the guy. It had been an accident. She tossed her chest and back pads at the growing pile of equipment. Cooper helmet with cage, jersey, neck guard, elbow pads, Koho gloves, pants, shin pads, girls' can, long underwear, not to mention Bauer skates, aluminum sticks, extra blades, and other assorted stuff made quite a sight.

Why hadn't Jimmy let her take her shot? Did he think she was that poor a player? She pulled on her jeans and T-shirt, then started stuffing her pile of equipment in her bag.

This had been their last game of the regular season. Losing to the Dynamos hadn't been the best way to end it, but they had still placed well enough in the standings to have secured a spot in the All City Championship.

The championship had been the dream of the whole team, and everyone had worked hard to get this far. Now all they had to do was win the playoff series and they'd take the coveted title.

No problem! They were the Forest Park Falcons. They could do it. She jammed the last of her stuff in her bag. They *would* do it.

Leigh came out of the washroom just as the other players were leaving.

"Nice play, Aberdeen," Jimmy said standing in her way. "Didn't you hear me when I told you to pass me the puck?" He was tall for his age and a lot stronger than the other boys in his class. Leigh noticed he'd slicked his pale blond hair back off his forehead, which somehow made him look older. A lot of the girls in her grade thought he looked like Brad Pitt. Yeah right, Leigh thought as she took a deep breath and squared her shoulders.

"I had a clear shot. I just needed the two defencemen blocked."

The rest of the team had gathered around them now.

"Well, on the Falcons, you do what the captain says." Jimmy moved in closer to her. "No hotshots trying to go for the glory and costing us the game instead!"

Just then Coach Stevenson came out of the dressing room. "Okay, that's enough, Jimmy. Leigh made a mistake. It happens to everyone. Next time she'll watch her stick in close quarters. Now, break it up." He waved the boys in the direction of the doors. "Your parents are waiting to get you guys home. Don't forget practice tomorrow night," he called to the retreating players.

The coach walked Leigh out. "Jimmy had a point, Leigh. We have to play as a team or we won't stand a chance. If you want to grandstand, you're on the wrong team. I don't know exactly what happened out there, but it looked like you wouldn't pass to Jimmy, lost control of the puck, then got angry and high-sticked that Dynamo player. That penalty cost us."

Leigh bit her lip. She wanted to tell the coach her side of things, but she didn't trust herself to speak. Coach Stevenson continued talking. "Don't take it so hard, Leigh. We're still in the playoffs. We're still going all the way." He smiled at Leigh. "Winning the City Championship would mean a lot to the club." She started to walk over to her dad. "Practice tomorrow at 7:00," the coach reminded her. "It's important."

Leigh winced at the reminder about the practice. She'd had a few problems juggling her schedule and as a result, she'd missed several practices. She knew they were part of playing on the team, but sometimes, when your mom and dad lived in two different houses, it was hard to fit everything in. She knew if she ditched her mom for hockey, there'd be trouble.

Her dad helped her with her equipment. "Bad break," was all he said, then he gave her a hug. "It was an excellent game till then. You played great, and so did the Fraser boy."

"Yeah, Robert kicked," Leigh agreed. "I wish I could stickhandle like him." She threw the gear she'd been carrying into the back of the car. "He told me he's from Mountain Mill, and says he can trace his Métis roots right back to a Hudson Bay trader who married a Cree lady in 1802. You're from around Mountain Mill, aren't you, Dad? Did you ever know the Frasers?" Leigh asked.

"I told you that was a long time ago. I don't know any of those people anymore." Her father started the engine, revving it loudly.

"But your family is Métis too and I thought—" Leigh began again.

"I don't want to talk about it," her dad said, cutting her off.

Her father always acted like that when Leigh mentioned anything about his Métis family. He never told the other engineers at the oil company he worked for or any of his friends about his roots. And since both she and her dad had such fair colouring, no one ever suspected they were Métis.

Her light brown hair and pale skin were even odder for Leigh considering her mom was a native Canadian, a member of the Tsuu T'ina nation. Her mother lived on the reserve close to the outskirts of Elliston. Leigh visited her mom on weekends and had a lot of fun with all her relatives there. Her mother was teaching her traditional native Fancy Dancing, and Leigh really enjoyed the colourful costumes and drumming. When she was with her mom, she felt "connected." To what she wasn't sure, but it was a good feeling anyway.

Leigh had never mentioned her mother to her

friends or told her dad about her Fancy Dancing. She knew her dad wouldn't like her doing Indian dancing. In fact, no one knew anything about that part of Leigh's life. It seemed to keep things simpler that way, especially with her dad. Not that she was ashamed of her Indian mother exactly…After all, she told herself, what would her teammates say? It was tough enough being the only girl player on a boys' team without adding more trouble.

Besides, it evened out because she kept her hockey playing secret from her mom. Her mom wanted Leigh to continue her dancing and would only worry about Leigh getting hurt if she knew about the hockey. Her mother had fallen from a horse when she was young and hurt her leg. She worried that something similar might happen to Leigh. Leigh had decided she was really doing her mom a favour by not telling her. It wasn't lying, exactly…

It was a good thing her parents never spoke to one another. It made keeping the two parts of her life separate and secret a lot easier. Hockey was something she shared with her dad and Fancy Dancing was with her mom. It wasn't easy, but her system had worked so far. Is everyone's life this complicated? Leigh wondered. She stared out the car window in silence as they rode home through the snow.

2 MYSTERY MESSAGE

The next day at school started out well, but soon went downhill. Leigh was in Ms. Martin's language arts class with her finished homework assignment on the desk in front of her. Then she noticed the other kids sneaking looks at her. She wondered what was going on. That's when she spotted Susan Crane, Jimmy's sister, talking to the boy at the desk ahead of her. The boy looked at Leigh, then quickly turned away.

Leigh stared down at her homework. She suddenly felt uncomfortable.

"Hey Leigh, how was the game last night?" Susan asked, showing just a few too many teeth when she smiled.

"We lost," Leigh said quietly.

"I heard the Falcons were real close to a win. In fact, wasn't it tied right down to the last minute of the game?" Susan asked sweetly.

"Yeah, that's right. Then the Dynamos rushed the net and scored," Leigh answered.

"'Rushed the net'? Isn't that a move you'd use when the other team is down a player?" Susan wasn't going to let up.

Leigh took a deep breath. "Yes. I was in the penalty box, making the Falcons a player short. The Dynamos used the opportunity to rush the Falcon net. They got lucky and scored," she finished lamely.

"My brother Jimmy said the Falcons could have won. You wouldn't pass him the puck. Jimmy's the Falcons' top scorer and captain of the team." She looked around the room at all the eavesdroppers, throwing out that tidbit of information in case they didn't already know.

"That's hockey. You win some and you lose some." Leigh pretended to make some changes on her homework papers.

Susan kept on. "My brother says the Falcons have a good shot at the city championship and he's going to make sure no female hotshot screws it up. He says girls don't belong on a boys' hockey team in the first place, especially one he's the captain of." She flipped her long blond hair over her shoulder.

Leigh clenched her fists. "Maybe your brother should try practising what he preaches. Other players are just as capable of scoring goals as he is, if he wouldn't bully them into giving up the puck." Her voice had gotten a little louder than she'd meant. Everyone was now openly staring at her and Susan.

"What's all this about?" Ms. Martin asked as she walked into the classroom. "Everyone take your seats."

Susan made a nasty face at Leigh and waltzed back to her desk. Leigh shuffled her homework papers.

By lunch, Leigh knew the rumour mill had beaten her to the cafeteria. At her school, hockey was king and anything connected with hockey was always a major topic. Several groups of kids began whispering as Leigh walked up to the food line.

She began to have that old feeling she used to get when she'd first signed up to play on the boys' team, that "I'm a freak for being the only girl on the team" feeling. Her dad had been proud of her, but everyone else had thought she was kind of strange. The thing was, she'd had no choice—there was no girls' team. If she wanted to play hockey, and she did more than anything, she had to play for the Falcons. She began studying the various lunch offerings, as if she couldn't hear the whispering and wouldn't care even if she could.

"Leigh, wait for me," a voice called from across the room.

Leigh turned and saw Tina Blake heading toward her. Tina was Leigh's best friend and sometime tutor. Her flaming red hair, which was cut by a barber in what Tina called a "number four razor buzz," was impossible to miss. Along with the hair, her friend's distinctive style of dress had always set Tina apart from the crowd—any crowd. Today she wore an old, dilapidated flak jacket she'd rescued from a garage sale and jeans that were more patches than pants. But the best part of her ensemble were her high tops with flashing lights in the heels that blinked on and off as she walked. Leigh grinned as Tina strode through the crowd toward her, paying no attention to the kids already standing in line.

"Hi Tina, you must be feeling awfully brave," Leigh said getting another tray for her friend.

"You mean all that talk about you blowing the game with the Dynamos? Don't worry, I don't think they'll stone you while I'm standing so close." She grinned at Leigh.

"Thanks for taking the chance." Leigh grabbed a chocolate milk for herself and an apple juice for Tina.

They headed for an empty table to eat their lunch. Tina had just begun telling Leigh about her killer math test that morning when Leigh spotted several Falcon players coming in, including Jimmy Crane. Leigh smiled and waved. A couple of the players started to wave back at her, but quickly pulled their hands down when Jimmy said something to them.

Leigh sat listening to Tina chatter on and ate her lunch in silence.

They'd almost finished when Leigh finally spoke up. "I'm going to have to be a combination of Mario Lemieux and Wayne Gretzky at practice tonight," she said, gulping the last of her milk. "It's the only thing I can do to make the guys forget about the Dynamos game."

"Tempest in a teapot," Tina said, grinning. "You can skate rings around those guys, Leigh. Don't let one little screw-up get you rattled. There'll be other games."

"Lets hope," Leigh replied, remembering what Susan had said about Jimmy fixing it so no girls played on his team.

Afternoon classes dragged by, but eventually the final bell rang and Leigh gathered up her books and went to find Tina. They always walked home together.

"Do you need any help with that math assignment?" Tina asked as they turned down their street. Her breath made frosty little clouds in the cold March air.

"Nope. I think I've got that stuff figured out," Leigh said as she kicked an icicle off the bottom of Mr. Weiser's fence with her boot. She loved the way the ice snapped off so cleanly.

"Hey, why don't you chow down at my place tonight? Grandma's making your favourite, her secret-recipe lasagna," Tina asked, taking aim at her own icicle just as Leigh's boot flashed out, finishing it off.

"I better not. My dad's going to be home for supper and I've got hockey practice later. Thanks anyway." Having cleared the fence of icicles, Leigh continued walking toward her house, her boots crunching on the snow. She suddenly grinned over at her friend. "But you could save me some leftovers."

"Deal." Tina grinned back.

Leigh waved goodbye as she turned in at her gate.

When Leigh got inside, the first thing she always did was play the messages on the answering machine. Her mom often called to say hi, or tell her a joke she'd heard, and it made Leigh feel good. Today she could use a funny joke.

She hit the play button, then went to the fridge to get the milk out.

The voice on the machine was muffled, as if someone had held a cloth over the receiver of the phone.

"You should take the hint, Aberdeen. Why don't you stay home and play with your dolls like a nice little girl and leave hockey to the guys? No one wants you on the Falcons' team." The voice stopped. Leigh stared at the machine. She couldn't place the strange voice, but the message was very clear.

3 ROUGH PLAY

The phone rang just as Leigh finished loading the dishwasher with the supper dishes. She stuffed the last dinner plate in and ran to grab it.

"Hi, it's me." Tina's voice boomed at her. "I snagged you a nice chunk of lasagna. I could bring it over now and tag along with you to the rink if you want."

Leigh put her hand over the mouthpiece. "Dad, I forgot to tell you I have a practice tonight at 7:00. It's Tina, she wants to come with us. Is that okay with you?"

"Leigh, you really have to give me more warning about your practices." Her dad looked at his watch and nodded. "She should come right over. We've got to leave in about ten minutes."

"Sounds good," Leigh said to Tina, "but we're leaving soon, so go to warp nine."

"Right, I'll beam over," Tina said, her voice muffled, "...just as soon as I finish dessert."

Leigh went to grab her hockey gear. She thought about the answering machine message again. If she told

Tina, she knew her friend would freak out. She'd want a full investigation, complete with DNA evidence.

Besides, Tina was probably right. This whole thing was just a tempest in a teapot. It would blow over as quickly as it had started.

★★★

The air in the rink felt crisp on Leigh's face as she skated through her warm-up drills. She liked the way her blades cut into the freshly finished ice surface. She felt ready to skate.

Most of the guys seemed to have gotten over the previous night's game. With the exception of Jimmy and a few of his friends, everyone acted normally to her. Leigh, gliding effortlessly backward down the ice, waved her stick at Tina who was watching in the stands. Her dad had dropped the girls off, saying he had a couple of errands to run but would be back for them later. Leigh knew he hated to miss her practice. She hadn't meant to forget to tell him about it.

Coach Stevenson blew his whistle to assemble the skaters.

"We're going to have a little scrimmage. You bunch," he motioned to half the players, "go grab red bibs from the bench. The rest of you form up."

The players set themselves up on the ice for a face-off. Leigh knew it wasn't a coincidence that Jimmy and his friends were all wearing red bibs.

Trevor Greene, a band-aid glued to the side of his face where he'd run into the edge of the goalpost, grinned at Jimmy as he pulled his red bib over his helmet. He was tall and thin for his age and wore his hair spiked straight up which made him look even taller. On skates, in his bright green Falcons uniform, he really looked like the Jolly Green Giant. "Ready for a little smash and bash?" he asked.

Jimmy grinned back. "You bet, buddy." Then he nodded toward Michael Denning who already had a bib on and was starting for centre ice where two more of Jimmy's pals were in position for the faceoff. "Mike and the rest of the first line are all set." He looked over at Leigh. "The rest of these Falcon wannabes can try and keep up." He made sure his voice was loud enough for Leigh to hear. The two boys laughed as they skated toward centre ice.

As he skated by her, Leigh noticed one of Michael's eyes had a bit of a shiner and wondered if he'd gotten it on the ice or off. Michael wasn't exactly the shy type and had always been what teachers called "a little aggressive"—kind of the same way the Terminator was a little aggressive.

Jimmy's remarks had been out of line. He'd always disliked her being on the team, right from the beginning, but she'd proved she could play. She glanced over at Robert Fraser, noticing he didn't have a bib on. This made her feel a lot better. Robert was not only one of the best hockey players Leigh knew, but he was really nice—for a boy. She waved at him and skated to centre ice. From what Jimmy had said, her side was going to need all the good players they could get.

The minute the puck hit the ice, Leigh knew it was going to be a rough practice. The puck had barely cleared centre ice when a red player checked her hard from behind. It was Michael Denning.

She went sprawling across the ice, feeling stupid. She hadn't expected the hit. Scrambling to her feet, she raced toward the action, which was already at the far end of the rink. As she came around behind the goal, Jimmy cut her off, shoving her savagely into the boards. The air rushed out of her lungs as she tried to cushion her crash.

"You just can't take a hint, can you, Aberdeen," he snarled as he skated away.

She leaned over, trying to catch her breath. The rest of the practice was grim. Leigh had to skate as hard and fast as she did in a real game just to stay away from Jimmy and his goons.

By the time the coach blew the final whistle, she was sore and tired. She caught a glimpse of Tina in the stands. Her friend was on her feet, heading quickly down to the ice exit.

"Are those guys nuts?" she yelled angrily.

"I'm fine, thanks for asking," Leigh replied as she slowly came off the ice.

"Is that ref blind?" Tina waved her arms in the air.

"Coach," Leigh said, wincing at a new bruise she'd just discovered.

"What?" Tina said, stopping her tirade long enough to look at Leigh.

"The coach was not calling the cheap shots. Maybe he thought it would be good for us to have a real game type of thing. You know, take no prisoners." They headed to the women's washroom.

"I think it stinks." Tina shoved the washroom door open for Leigh. It hit the door stop with a bang and bounced back, smacking Tina hard in the chest. "Arrgh!" She gave the door another shove, this time not quite so hard.

"Maybe you should give up hockey for the rest of the season. Start again fresh next year," Tina said as she watched her friend pack up her stuff.

Leigh stopped what she was doing and stared at Tina. "Are you crazy? The championship's in a couple of weeks."

"I know, but things are getting really ugly. It was like a shopping mall the Saturday before Christmas out there. Next season, Jimmy will be in another division. You won't have to worry about being nuked by one of your own players." Tina was serious.

"Jimmy may be captain, but I'm not going to let him bully me off the team." Leigh grabbed the handles on her huge equipment bag." Come on, Dad's probably waiting."

After the gruelling practice, Leigh's muscles ached at the strain of hauling the heavy bag. Finally giving in, she had Tina grab one of the handles while she pulled on the other. By the time the girls made it to the front doors of the arena, Leigh's dad already had the car trunk open. "How'd it go?" he asked, taking the bag from the girls and stowing it in the trunk.

"Okay," Leigh said flatly.

"Brutal," Tina volunteered. "Those guys were out for blood."

Leigh's dad looked at her questioningly.

"It was just a little rough, Dad. Everybody's getting really pumped about the championship, so they're trying a little harder." She did up her seatbelt.

"The Mafia should have such enforcers," Tina mumbled as she climbed into the back seat.

4 POISON PINK POST-IT

After school the next day, Leigh decided the best way to loosen up after the rough practice was to head down to the nearby neighbourhood rink and do a little free skating. She checked the answering machine when she got home—no nasty messages—then grabbed her skates and headed out.

The afternoon was warm and sunny with the promise of spring on the west breeze. Leigh sat on a bench by the rink and watched the skaters for a while. The little kids were comical as they pushed their chairs around the ice to keep from falling down.

As Leigh pulled her skates on, she noticed Susan Crane arrive with several of her friends. They were all wearing similar skating outfits. Leigh thought they looked wimpy. One girl even had a fluffy white muff that she stuffed her hands into as she primly skated in tidy figure eights.

But it was Susan who caught Leigh's eye. When she glided effortlessly across the ice, Leigh could see she knew what she was doing. Her strong legs took her through a series of smooth, graceful movements which ate up the ice surface with no effort. She'd be wicked on a hockey team, Leigh thought as she watched Susan skate. No one could keep up with her.

When the girls took a break, Leigh worked her way over to the knot of pink and white outfits.

"You can really skate, Susan," she began awkwardly.

Susan looked at her icily. "I compete in figure skating competitions all the time. Of course I can skate," she answered, rolling her eyes.

"Yeah, well, you've got some good moves. Have you ever thought about joining the Falcons?" Leigh asked.

All the girls stopped talking and stared at Leigh like she had at least two heads.

"You mean play hockey?" Susan asked incredulously.

"We could always use a good skater," Leigh went on lamely. "You know, in case you get bored with figure skating."

Susan gave her blond head a toss and laughed. The sound was artificial, like the laugh of a soap opera star.

"I don't think so," she said in a voice dripping with sarcasm. She moved off smoothly with her friends following in her wake like so many perfectly pink ducklings.

As Leigh finished her skate, she thought she caught Susan eyeing her a couple of times. But when Leigh looked directly at her, Susan would turn away.

★★★

Leigh was watching TV when her dad came home.

"Hi, honey." He smiled at her mischievously. "Karl Leitz needed someone to take a couple of Calgary Flames vs. Edmonton Oilers tickets off his hands. How could I refuse to help my old friend out?" He held two tickets up. "I don't suppose you'd like to go to a game with me tonight?"

"True story!" Leigh said, jumping up from the couch.

"If that means you'd like to go with your old dad, then I guess we're on." He started upstairs to change. "We can grab a bite to eat on the way downtown if you want."

"Sweet!" Leigh exclaimed with a grin, "I already ate the leftovers Tina brought for an after-school snack. I could really use a hamburger and fries."

"I'm glad to see you're not worried about your weight like so many girls your age," he laughed.

"Hey, I'm a growing kid," Leigh protested. "Besides, I'm too young to worry about all that figure stuff, especially since I don't have one yet," she giggled.

★★★

The game was an exciting one—lots of action with some really slick plays. Leigh watched as the two teams prepared for a faceoff in Oiler territory. As she watched the play unfold, something about it seemed familiar. She couldn't put her finger on it, then suddenly she had it figured out. It was the same one the Flames had used twice before that night, and both times it had worked great. It wasn't so much a tricky play as a fast, sneaky one. With a few changes it might even work for the Falcons…Yes! It didn't require super tough puck handling or much muscle, just good teamwork and timing. They could do it. The more she thought about it, the more excited she became. She could hardly wait to tell the guys. This was going to be great.

★★★

The sudden clamour of the final class bell jolted Leigh out of her favourite daydream. It was the one which involved her, hockey, and an NHL scout who was trying to sign her to a multi-million dollar deal. She sat up at her desk and closed her notebook.

"Man, am I glad that's over," Tina sighed, slamming her text shut. "I can never remember who's the good guy, Wolfe or Montcalm."

"I guess that depended on which side you were on." Leigh grinned as she packed up her books.

The girls joined the noisy crush of kids heading out into the hall.

Leigh planned what she'd do when she got home.

She decided she'd better practise her Fancy Dancing for a while. Her mom had shown her a new move last weekend and Leigh wanted to go over it before she forgot.

She would just have to make sure she finished before her dad arrived. He hated the native drum music she used for dancing.

As Leigh walked up to her locker, a bright pink Post-it stuck to the door grabbed her attention.

"Hey, what's that?" Tina joked. "A secret admirer leaving you love notes?"

"Yeah, right," Leigh said, peeling the little piece of pink paper off the locker. She looked at the messy printing.

"GET OFF THE TEAM WHILE YOU STILL CAN" was spelled out in block letters.

"Oh my gosh," Tina said reading the note over Leigh's shoulder. "Who sent that little number?"

"I don't know. Probably the same jerk who left the message on my answering machine," Leigh replied without thinking.

Tina pounced on the slip. "What message?"

Feeling a little sheepish for not telling Tina in the first place, Leigh explained briefly about the phone message.

"You've got to tell somebody, Leigh—the principal, the police," Tina said worriedly. "This is out of control."

"I don't want to make waves. I think if I ignore it,

the guy will get tired of doing these stupid things."

"Yeah, sure," Tina said, shaking her head. "And what if he doesn't? What's this psycho going to do next? I could tell you about some scenes from movies that will curl your hair," she added helpfully.

"It's okay, Tina. Don't worry," Leigh said smiling reassuringly. "Anybody makes any moves on me, I'll check him so hard he'll think a tank rolled over him." Leigh stuffed the note in her jeans.

5 STREET FIGHT

Saturday morning, Leigh awoke to the delicious smells of bacon, eggs, hashbrowns, and fried bread. She could hear her mother humming in the kitchen as she prepared breakfast. Leigh smiled to herself as she snuggled down under the warm covers. Her mom's house on the reserve was so small and cozy, she always felt at home.

From the way the sunlight was slanting into her room, Leigh knew it was still early. She stretched and yawned. Today, she and her mother were going to be busy. They were going into the city to the museum where there was a large exhibit of rare and beautiful aboriginal dresses. She and her mother hoped to be inspired by the colours and designs.

Her mom was making a new dress for Leigh to wear in her traditional dance. It would be the first one of her very own and Leigh had given it a lot of thought. She'd decided she'd like the colours to match her favourite hockey team, the Calgary Flames. Her mom was leaning more toward sky blue and white. Today, they'd make a decision.

First, however, they would go to the meeting hall where each Saturday, all the young people on the reserve gathered to learn from the elders.

The boys were taught ancient woodworking skills as they made bark canoes, pipes, and carvings. While they worked, they listened to the elders talk of how things were done in the old days.

In the beginning, it had seemed strange to Leigh to have the boys separated from the girls, since she was just as interested as the boys in building canoes, but the elders had been very firm.

Leigh didn't think it would have been polite to point out that this was the twenty-first century, and girls could do anything guys could. Besides, there would be time later to learn how to build a birchbark canoe.

One of the things Leigh liked best was to sit in on the stories and retelling of old legends. Here she learned how a sweet grass ceremony could fit in naturally with a world of computers, the Internet, and video games.

The girls busied themselves with beading, traditional cooking, and of course, Leigh's favourite, dancing. By ten o'clock, the building would be alive with the sounds of drumming, dancing, and lots of laughter as young and old exchanged points of view on every subject a twelve-year-old or a seventy-year-old could think of.

It made Leigh "smile with her heart" in anticipation of the fun she would have at class. Jumping out of bed, she dressed quickly and went to join her mother for breakfast.

"Good morning, sleepy head," her mother greeted her as Leigh sat at the table. "Ready for our big day?"

Leigh grinned at her mom and reached for the stack of steaming pancakes she'd just noticed tucked between the tray of delicious-smelling bacon and the bowl of crisp, brown fried bread.

"You bet, Mom." Leigh nodded eagerly. "It's going to be a great day."

They finished breakfast and started walking toward the meeting hall. It was a bright morning with a warm chinook breeze blowing out of the west. The sun glinted off the snow, making Leigh blink at what she'd always called "frozen diamond dust."

"You can change into a dress for the museum when we go home to get the car," her mother said as she walked beside Leigh. She had a peculiar gait—one leg didn't bend right because of the accident.

Leigh groaned. "A *dress*? I have to wear a dumb dress?" She would feel like a big geek wearing a dress. No self-respecting kid wore anything but jeans on Saturday.

Her mother gave her one of her looks. Discussion closed.

The dancing was great. Leigh was finally beginning to feel as though she were a part of the music as she moved her feet to the beat of the drum. Her mom's professional dance group, Wind Dancer, was also practising, but not with the younger girls. They were too good and too busy rehearsing the intricate steps Leigh's mom had shown them. Every once in a while Leigh would catch her mom watching her as Leigh went through the routine she'd been working on. Her mom had a kind of serious look on her face, like she did when she was marking school papers from her grade-six class.

Finally the drums fell silent, and the dancers' feet stopped. It had been a good practice. Leigh knew she'd danced well. It was a good feeling.

"You're really coming along, Leigh." Her mother smiled as they walked along the snowy road on their way back to the house. "I think you've been rehearsing at home." She slid Leigh a sidelong look.

Leigh knew she was wondering about Leigh's dad. If Leigh had practised when he was around, there would have been trouble.

"Yeah, I dance after school before dad comes home," she offered in way of an answer and an explanation. "It works out pretty good because it gives me a kind of mental break before I have to do my homework." They continued on in silence.

They didn't discuss her dad much. Her mom and dad had been divorced for a long time now. Leigh never knew why, but she suspected it had something to do with the way her dad felt about his roots. Whenever she asked either of her parents what happened, they'd both answer that they had married very young and people change.

★★★

Leigh stood uncomfortably beside her mom as they waited at the entrance to the museum gallery where the costume exhibit was being shown. She had on a baby blue dress in something her mom called a "Dotted Swiss" material, with white stockings, white patent leather shoes, and an honest-to-goodness bow in her hair. Unbelievable! She was way past geeky, but her mom thought she looked lovely.

Leigh caught a glimpse of herself in a mirror across the hall. Yup, she agreed, "lovely" is the only word to describe this getup.

The exhibit was really great. The museum had displays of different tribal dress for the plains Indians, from before the Hudson's Bay traders brought European glass beads to modern-day dress, including a model in a suit and tie.

Leigh and her mom had laughed at the dark-skinned mannequin in the tailored suit. He looked as unnatural as a cowboy forced into a bright pink tutu. The suit just didn't look practical—especially since the museum had placed the poor guy in a diorama depicting rolling prairie with a ghost herd of buffalo charging across the painted clouds in the background.

The ladies' costumes were much more interesting. The traditional dyes using barks and minerals had retained much of their colour. The bone needles used for sewing and the porcupine quills in the decoration were especially interesting.

The modern dresses had some interesting combinations of beading, colour, and intricate design. Some of the designs caught Leigh's attention, but the one she'd thought up herself was still her favourite.

Finally, after viewing the extraordinary colours and variety used in the dresses, Leigh convinced her mom that the bright reds and oranges she'd picked for her dress would work. The design would just have to be subtle enough that it wouldn't look garish, and Leigh's pattern was exactly that. Her mom was skeptical, but had agreed in the end. "Let's go out for supper," her mom suggested as they were preparing to leave the museum.

"Awesome!" Leigh grinned. "I'm starving. It's been years since breakfast."

The sky was grey and fresh snow was falling as they pushed through the heavy doors. Leigh glanced around in the dull afternoon light. Suddenly, as she stood staring down the street, fear gripped her stomach. Jimmy Crane, with Trevor, Michael, and two other hockey buddies in tow, was heading straight toward them.

She wished she could melt into a puddle on the sidewalk.

"You wait here, I'll go get the car," her mother suggested, unaware of Leigh's rising panic. "It's been snowing for a while and I don't want you to get your shoes wet walking through this slush. I'll only be a minute." She headed for the crosswalk to the parking lot across the street.

Leigh pulled the collar of her coat up around her face, but it was too late.

"Gee, Aberdeen," Jimmy called sarcastically. "Don't you look precious."

Leigh hoped her mother wouldn't hear him and turn back.

"You should wear that getup to the next Falcons game instead of your uniform," Jimmy continued relentlessly. "Maybe you could distract the other team with your clown outfit while we score some goals." All five guys started laughing as they crowded around.

"I don't know, Jimmy, the blue does bring out the colour in her eyes," Trevor offered as he grinned at her. He still had the band-aid on his face, but now it was dirty and starting to peel up at the edges.

"Yeah, yeah, go ahead, take your best shots," Leigh said in way of a lame defence. "But," she held her head up, "before you get too mouthy, remember the point scorers for the Falcons." She frowned as though trying to recall the elusive names. "Oh yes, Jimmy Crane tops the list," she gave Jimmy a quick toothy grin, "then who comes next?" She shook her head, paused and smiled sweetly. "Oh, I just remembered, it's me. I think if you check the record, you'll find I have the number two spot by a mile." She looked around at the group of boys. They stopped laughing and even looked a little sheepish. Trevor nudged Michael self-consciously.

"Yeah," Jimmy said, suddenly flustered at how Leigh had turned the conversation around. "Maybe, Aberdeen, but not from goals." He finished smugly, "I'm the top goal scorer."

"Sure, we know how you like to score, Jimmy." She shot him a knowing look. "But assist points are just as good in my book, as long as it's a Falcon player scoring."

Leigh could see her mother watching her from across the street. She was hesitating before getting into the car, looking like she might call out to Leigh, or worse, come back for her.

"And now," Leigh said quickly, "I gotta go." She started to make her way out of the circle of boys.

"What's your hurry, Aberdeen? Afraid your pretty girl clothes will get all wet with the snow?" Jimmy asked. He moved in front of her, blocking her way.

"Move, Jimmy," Leigh warned through clenched teeth. She could see her mother starting back toward the street.

Jimmy just folded his arms. "Or what? You going to stomp your pretty little shoes and start crying?" The other guys snickered.

Leigh could feel herself getting angry.

"Let her go," Trevor said, pulling his unzipped coat closer around him. "It's freezing out here. I want to get going."

Jimmy didn't move. Leigh's mom was at the curb now and about to jaywalk across to her. She had to do something.

"Yeah, let me go," Leigh said and shoved Jimmy with all her strength.

The sidewalk was slippery and Jimmy hadn't been prepared for Leigh's hefty push. He overbalanced and fell backward, hitting the soggy ground with a splat.

Leigh bolted across the street before any of the boys could react. She could hear Trevor and Michael laughing as Jimmy struggled to his feet.

"What was that all about?" her mother asked as Leigh grabbed her mother's arm and turned her back toward the car.

"Oh, nothing. Just some kids from school commenting on my lovely outfit. I told you I looked like a geek. The guys were just confirming it." She glanced back at the boys who were still laughing as they walked off. All of them except Jimmy. The butt of his jeans was stained dark with the melted slush. He looked furious. Leigh slid into the car and reached for her safety belt. "Where should we eat?" she asked brightly, hoping to steer her mother onto another train of thought. Leigh desperately hoped her mom hadn't heard any of the talk about her playing hockey.

It seemed to work.

"I don't know. What do you feel like?" she asked as she manoeuvred the old Toyota onto the deserted street.

"I was thinking Chinese," Leigh offered as she started to relax.

"Sounds good. I know a great little place…" Her mom was concentrating on driving now, and Leigh knew everything was okay.

She sighed and settled back in her seat. Calmer, Leigh watched the big lazy flakes of snow hit the windshield as they drove on into the late afternoon twilight.

6 BENCHED!

Things calmed down during the week following the museum incident. Jimmy and his friends had acted normally—for them, anyway.

Even at hockey practice, the goon squad hadn't tried to skate her into the boards. This was a big relief to Leigh, especially as Tina and her dad had watched the practice.

"Wait till you see how they have Leigh targeted for extinction," Tina had said on the way to the rink.

"If it looks out of control, I'll have to step in, Leigh," her dad had warned.

Wild comments like that made Leigh relieved that things had gone smoothly. If her dad had seen how she had been pummelled during that killer practice, he'd have raised a real stink.

The rest of the week dragged by, but finally Friday arrived. Tonight they began the playoff series to see who would be the new city champs. The top four teams from the regular season would compete.

The Dynamos had finished first, then the Falcons, followed by the Red Hots and finally the Cougars. That meant the Dynamos would play the Cougars, and the Falcons would be matched up against the Red Hots.

The winners of these games would play each other for the overall championship.

Leigh was sure the Falcons could go all the way. Well, almost sure.

She hadn't even had to invent an excuse to tell her mom for not coming over. Her mom's group, Wind Dancer, had an important rehearsal and Leigh had volunteered to come over on Saturday morning instead. It worked out perfectly.

"Come on, Tina, quit dragging," Leigh said as she hurried on her way home. She wanted to sneak in a quick dance practice to calm her pre-game jitters.

"What's your hurry?" Tina asked as she eyed a perfect row of icicles hanging off the bottom of a wrought iron fence they were passing. Before Leigh could even think of beating her to it, Tina's boot shot out and snapped the first one off. She smiled in victory, then noticed Leigh hadn't even tried for it.

"Look, Tina," Leigh said continuing past the waiting icicles without so much as a glance, "I have all this stuff to do at home before the game tonight and I don't want to be late." She wanted to tell her friend about her dancing, but the timing was wrong. It would open a big can of worms that Leigh didn't want to get into right now. She really should tell Tina about everything. Maybe she wouldn't feel so pulled apart if she had someone to talk to, and Tina was cool—she was the best. Leigh was sure she'd understand.

"Look, I'll see you at the game, okay?" Leigh said turning in at her gate and giving Tina a quick wave goodbye.

"Whatever," Tina said with a sigh and continued toward her own house next door.

Slamming the front door, Leigh kicked off her boots and dropped her coat and books. She decided to grab a quick snack before starting her dancing. When her mom and dad had divorced and her mom had moved back to the reserve, coming home to an empty house had bothered Leigh; now she was used to it. She actually liked the time between school and dad's arrival every evening. She could have her music dialled up as loud as she wanted with no hassles.

Walking into the kitchen, she noticed the light flashing on the answering machine. Without thinking, Leigh hit the play button and headed over to the cupboard.

The voice made her stop in her tracks.

"This is your last warning. Get off the team. We don't want a girl on the Falcons." It was the same strange voice as before.

Leigh listened, confused. The practice had been great. The team was playing like a well-oiled machine. They'd all worked hard and later, after practice, everyone had been laughing and joking. Why would anyone on the Falcons want to get rid of her now when they were going into the finals?

The back door slammed.

"Hi, it's me," Tina called.

Leigh hit the erase button before the machine had a chance to finish playing. She didn't want Tina to hear this nut and start over-reacting. Anyway, she couldn't do anything about the message now, and as long as all the creep did was phone her, Leigh decided she could handle it.

"I thought I'd help you with the 'stuff' you ditched me for so you could come over to my place sooner," she said stepping out of her oversized snow boots.

"What are you talking about?" Leigh asked, puzzled. "And I didn't ditch you," she added a little guiltily.

"Your dad called to say he had a job that had to be done at warp speed, so he asked if you could eat at our house. He said he'd be home in time to take you to the game, though. Didn't you get your message?" she asked, looking over at the whirring machine.

Leigh glanced at the answering machine which was just finishing erasing the last of the messages. What if the creep called back while Tina was here? Maybe they shouldn't hang around. Tina would get all wired and want to tell Leigh's dad about everything.

He'd get excited and there'd be a big blow-up.

"Ah, yeah. Sure. What's your mom making? Lasagna,

maybe?" she said hopefully.

"Nope, hamburger stew and some kind of smashed potatoes," Tina said, making a face.

"Let's head out now. I can get my hockey gear later." Leigh ran back to the front hall to reclaim her boots.

"What about your important stuff?" Tina asked confused.

"It'll wait," Leigh said, stuffing her double stockinged feet into her boots.

"Okay by me," Tina said, putting her own boots back on. "But as your best friend, I have to tell you, you're acting pretty weird."

Leigh ignored her and clomped back to the front hall for her coat, not bothering to take her boots off again.

"Ready, let's go," she said, pulling her toque out of her pocket and jamming it down over her ears.

Tina nodded. "You ready for the game?" she asked, heading back outside.

Leigh grinned at her friend. "Yeah. The Falcons can beat the Hotshots. No worries." No worries, she repeated to herself and followed Tina into the dark backyard.

★★★

The rink was buzzing with excitement as Leigh sat on the bench waiting for the coach to call his starting line-up. She always felt nervous before a game, but it was a good kind of nervous.

"Jimmy, Todd, Raj, Trevor, and Robert—you guys start," the coach called, looking at his clipboard.

Leigh couldn't believe it. The second most important game of the season and she wasn't starting? She was one of the Falcons' best skaters. It was odd, but maybe the coach was saving her for a fresh rush later in the game.

The game began fast and continued without letting up. The Red Hots weren't going down without a fight. Leigh noticed she wasn't getting her usual number of shifts, but when she was on the ice, she skated as hard as she could.

When an over-excited fan threw his soft drink on the ice, the ref stopped the game until it was cleaned up. Leigh moved over beside Coach Stevenson. "Excuse me, Coach," she interrupted.

He looked down at her. "What's the problem, Aberdeen?"

"It's just you usually play me more. Is there something wrong with my skating tonight?" she asked, puzzled. She probably shouldn't question a coach, but she'd only been on the ice about half her usual time.

The coach tapped his clipboard with his pen. "Look, to tell you the truth, I've had some complaints about your attitude. A few of the parents are concerned you might jeopardize tonight's game. It's too important to have any dissension in the ranks. Each player here has worked very hard and put the team first on their list of priorities. The Falcons are a good team and deserve to win the championship."

"But—" Leigh started to protest.

"That's my decision. Besides, you've had as much ice time as a lot of the other players." He turned back to his clipboard.

Leigh made her way back to her chunk of bench. He was right. She had played the same amount as many of the other players. But this was a crucial game and it was hard for her to just wait her turn. Maybe she was overreacting...She sat and refocused on the game.

The tension in the rink was high. More than three-quarters of the game was over and no one had scored. Both goalies were playing flawlessly.

When one of the Hotshots got a breakaway, the crowd went wild. Leigh, sitting on the edge of the bench, watched breathlessly. Suddenly, Robert and Michael appeared on either side of the speeding Red Hot forward. With a great team play, Michael checked the forward, while Robert stripped him of the puck.

Turning, Robert headed back down the ice. The play looked slick, especially with Robert's smooth stickhandling. The Falcons didn't score, but kept the puck in the Red Hots' end for the next faceoff.

Jimmy was sitting next to Leigh, as impatient as she was to get back out on the ice.

"We need an edge," he said to no one in particular as he watched the puck being passed back and forth between two Falcons. "Something new and racy the Hotshots haven't seen before."

Leigh agreed, and she knew just the play.

"Jimmy, I've got a play that's exactly what we need right now." She looked at him excitedly. The three-man play she'd seen the Flames use would work perfectly in this situation. Quickly, she told Jimmy her idea. She and Jimmy would set the whole thing up, passing the puck to the blue line so fast, the Red Hots wouldn't know where it was. Then Jimmy would fire it into the Red Hots' end where Robert would intercept and blam, the puck would be blasted past the goalie before he knew what hit him. It was sure-fire.

Jimmy listened in silence, then shook his head. "You've got to be kidding, Aberdeen. That will never work. Too artsy. It sounds like something my sister would use in her figure skating. Forget it. You see plays like that in the NHL for a reason."

Leigh just looked at him. He wasn't even willing to try the play. The clock was ticking away. Maybe Coach Stevenson would think differently. She looked over at the coach just as he pointed at her and Jimmy for a line switch. Too late now, she thought as her skates hit the ice moving.

The pace was furious. Leigh could see Trevor intercept a pass and turn for the net. Jimmy moved up behind him and yelled something at Trevor. Trevor suddenly passed Jimmy the puck. Leigh checked one of the

Red Hots into the boards on her way by as she headed over to give Jimmy some help. Jimmy began a series of dekes and dodges which looked impressive, but his stickhandling could barely keep up with his skating. He cut hard left, a little too hard, misjudged the distance and clipped the edge of the boards with his skate. He spun into the boards with a loud thump. The puck ricocheted and headed back down the ice toward the Falcon net. Leigh pushed hard to turn and intercept the puck before it crossed the blue line. She just managed to grab it with her stick, but knew she was way out of position to do any good. Then she spotted Robert in the open down ice.

Using all her strength, she fired the puck toward him. Robert met the puck, zipped behind the Red Hots' goal, came out the other side in a great-looking wraparound, and slammed the puck home. The arena erupted in an explosion of cheers. Even diehard Red Hots fans couldn't help but be impressed with a play like that!

The final score was Falcons 1, Red Hots 0. The Falcons were thumping each other on the back and waving their sticks. Now all they had to do was beat the winner of the Dynamo-Cougar game and the championship was theirs. This was their year and, Leigh thought, she was going to be a part of it. She felt elated.

Everyone was laughing and slapping Robert on the back. She even got her share of congratulatory pats on the top of her helmet. She smiled as the team filed back to the dressing room while the crowd cheered. The only person who didn't seem pleased was Jimmy.

"You played first-rate, honey," her dad said hugging her as she came out of the women's washroom.

"Thanks, Dad." Leigh dropped her heavy bag on the floor.

"I also heard a bit of news you'll want to know," he added.

"Like what? Some scout for a farm team was in the stands tonight and wants to sign me?" Leigh joked.

"Not this game, honey. Actually, I heard who you'll be playing for the championship," he answered too casually.

"Who? I mean which one—the Cougars or the Dynamos?" she asked, already suspecting the answer.

"The Dynamos. They beat the Cougars 8–0," he answered, confirming her suspicion.

She thought about the prospect of playing the Dynamos, then grinned.

"No worries, Dad. We'll kick their Dynamo butt." She smiled up at him. "We're ready."

"I can see that, and to celebrate tonight's victory, how about we go grab a pizza?" he asked.

Tina and her family appeared at the end of the hall.

"Did I hear someone mention pizza?" Tina asked, grinning.

"Everyone's heading over to Tony's. We could go

there," Leigh suggested.

"Sounds good to me," her dad agreed as he picked up Leigh's equipment bag.

"Great! I'm starved," Tina said, already heading for the arena doors.

★★★

The pizza really hit the spot. Leigh was ravenous. Her legs felt like rubber as she sat in the booth at the pizza parlour. The room was filled with Falcon players and friends. Every table was rehashing the game and discussing how best to beat the Dynamos. News travelled fast.

After the pizza, Tina and her family had to leave. Leigh and her dad stayed until Leigh finished her second piece of cherry pie.

From the booth behind, Leigh heard laughter, then Jimmy's familiar voice.

"You guys are dead wrong. I would have had that goal if Aberdeen hadn't interfered on the play." Jimmy sounded bitter.

Leigh swallowed her bite of pie.

She heard Trevor Greene's voice. "Maybe you should learn how to turn before you try any tight manoeuvres, Jimmy." The other guys at the table laughed.

"I'm telling you, Aberdeen crowded me into the boards. I could see her coming. She didn't leave me any room to turn." He was speaking loud enough for Leigh's dad to hear now. His face went still as he listened to the conversation.

Leigh saw his lips take on that thin line they always did when he was angry. She knew what that look meant. He stood up, never glancing at her, and walked to the booth behind them.

He stood in front of Jimmy. "I heard what you said about my daughter. I think you'd better stop and think before you start blaming your mistakes on another player. Leigh was on her way to run interference for you with the other team's defence. All you had to do was get your bearings and head for the goal." He shook his head. "You're supposed to be the captain." He stared hard at Jimmy. "Maybe you should start acting like one."

He came back to their table, where Leigh was sitting poking at her pie with her fork. She could feel a burning flush of embarrassment creeping up past her ears.

Leigh heard the guys getting ready to leave. They'd know it if she hid under the table. Besides, her face was so red, they'd spot the glow anyway. She pretended not to see them as they filed past her table.

She pushed her unfinished pie away. Suddenly she wasn't very hungry anymore.

7 HOMEMADE FRIENDS

It was one of those days when even math class went well. The win against the Red Hots had turned everyone's championship fever on. There had already been two pep rallies at school proclaiming the Falcons the next city champs. Feeling great, Leigh was heading down the jammed hallway toward her locker when Tina caught up with her.

"Ready for lunch? I'm so hungry I could eat vegetables," she said grinning at Leigh. "How'd French go?"

"*Très bien*," Leigh said and giggled. "*Je suis très* hungry too."

Just then Robert and his newly acquired crowd of well-wishers moved past Leigh and Tina. Since the game, the name "Robert Fraser" had become a buzzword. He was a genuine hero. There was always a gang of kids around him, telling him what a great job he did at the game. Robert would just nod and smile shyly.

"It's great the Falcons' star spotlight is finally on someone besides Jimmy Crane. Robert deserves some of that glitter. He was really something at the game," Tina said, watching the hockey hero, then she added with a sigh, "I never noticed how dark brown his eyes are, have you?" she asked Leigh as she tracked Robert down the hall. "Or how tall and darkly handsome he is, even out of his hockey uniform. And have you checked out how he pulls that shiny black hair into that super-looking ponytail?"

Leigh rolled her eyes. Tina was positively gushing.

"Can't say any of that was too high on my list of priorities," Leigh said, following Tina's gaze.

"Did you know he's a Métis?" she asked, pronouncing the "s" sound.

"Yes, I heard something about that," Leigh responded casually.

"I think it's too cool. He has this really great family history with Indians and fur traders and all that. Why can't I have something historically awesome about my family?" she asked, as though Leigh had all the answers to the hard questions.

Leigh thought a moment. "Because you weren't around when your great, great, great grandpa met your great, great, great grandma. You end up who you are because of a bunch of people you never met."

Tina stopped and grinned. "Hey, when you put it like that, I guess it's not my fault I'm related to my noxious animal brothers. Cool."

"Sort of," Leigh said hesitantly. Sometimes Tina had

a habit of putting her own spin on things.

"Speaking of noxious things," Tina went on, "guess what I heard about Mr. Jimmy Crane?" She deftly side-stepped a couple of kids barrelling down the hall past them.

"I'll bite, what?" Leigh asked, reaching for the door on her locker.

"Well, you'll never believe this," Tina began conspiratorially. "The grapevine tells me Jimmy Crane isn't the super jock we all know and love just because he likes hockey. It seems his dad is pushing him to be some kind of NHL Superstar. If he doesn't score every game, he's in big trouble with his dad, yelling, grounding, the whole deal."

Leigh stopped putting her books away. "You're kidding! Mr. Crane is always really enthusiastic about Jimmy's playing, but I thought he was just being a hockey dad."

"Don't start pulling the hankies out for old Jimmy just yet. The other part of the deal is, for every goal Jimmy scores, his dad gives him twenty bucks! And he doesn't care how Jimmy gets them. A little thing like sportsmanship is no reason for Jimmy not to skate right over any kid—on either team—in order to get the puck." Her eyes narrowed into Tina's version of a sinister look. "I tell you, it's blood money, just like working for the mob." She drew her finger across her throat in a grim gesture.

Leigh winced. "I wouldn't go that far. Lots of kids get incentives to play, maybe not as generous as Jimmy's, but something. It must put killer pressure on him. Every game he's got to be a winner or else." She shoved the last of her books into her locker. "Besides, Jimmy does work hard and he's done a good job as captain." She slammed her locker shut and stopped.

Susan Crane was standing right beside them at her locker, which was next to Leigh's. She was staring into it like it was a new video game. Her face was crimson. Without saying a word, she closed her locker door and walked away.

"Did you see her face?" Tina asked. "She was really ticked. I bet she runs straight to her stupid brother and reports what she heard. Who knew she'd be eavesdropping? Besides, the info I got came from a very reliable source, so she really shouldn't be so mad about someone simply repeating the truth, right?"

Leigh didn't say anything. After a moment, she shrugged her shoulders, "Let's head down to the cafeteria before all the edible stuff gets taken."

Tina fell in beside her as Leigh started down the hall.

★★★

The cafeteria was jammed when they arrived with few spots left open. The noise level was similar to that at a rock concert.

"What a mob," Tina complained, putting a helping of spaghetti on her tray and grabbing the last apple juice. "I'll go save us a couple of seats." She handed the cashier her money and kept going. Leigh continued looking for the right change to pay for her alleged meatloaf.

As Leigh picked up her tray, she noticed Susan coming through the doors. Tina was frantically signalling from a table in the corner. Leigh started to make her way through the noisy throng.

They'd just started eating, when Leigh looked up to see Susan, without her usual gaggle of girls, searching for a place to sit. The only available seat left was beside Tina.

Susan headed toward their table. She set her tray down and took the remaining empty spot. "Can I sit here?"

The girls shrugged. "Sure," Leigh said.

"Quite the crowd," Susan said, as she opened her chocolate milk.

"Yeah," Tina replied with a mouthful of spaghetti. She glanced at Leigh. The tension level had just gone way up.

Leigh busied herself trying to cut her meatloaf. "You'd think the kitchen staff had ordered take-out food the way everything's disappeared."

"That, or they hired an actual cook instead of the usual home-ec dropouts," Susan said, working on her own mystery food.

All three girls looked at each other, then Leigh felt a giggle start.

"You're right about that," Tina agreed, a long piece of spaghetti hanging out of the corner of her mouth, which wiggled when she talked. Susan took one look at Tina and tried to suppress her own laughter.

"What's so funny, you guys? I know I haven't got spinach stuck in my teeth, I'm eating spaghetti," she said, looking from Leigh to Susan.

This sent Leigh and Susan into fits of giggles.

"We can see that," Leigh said.

Susan handed Tina a napkin. "This is for your doggie bag," she said with a straight face.

Tina wiped her mouth, saw the spaghetti mess, then continued wiping until all the evidence was cleaned up. "That's mature, you guys," she said, trying to hide her grin behind her napkin. "I hope I can return the favour one day."

She faked a hurt look, but couldn't quite get it right. "I suppose it could have been worse. I could have had a spinach salad as an appetizer," she said, grinning broadly and showing her front teeth.

The tension had evaporated. Lunch continued with various suggestions being offered as to why the cafeteria was so overcrowded. By the time they'd finished, the girls were giggling conspiratorially over the mystery of the strange attraction to the mutant food.

As they were leaving the cafeteria, Susan stopped Leigh.

"I heard what you said about Jimmy at your locker. Despite everything, he really does love hockey. It's important to him, not just because of my dad either." She looked down at the books she was holding. "I appreciate your sticking up for him. I think he's done a great job as captain too, and I hope people remember that."

"Hey, I'm a Falcon. We've got to stick together, especially now." She smiled at Susan who nodded and smiled back.

"Let's go, Leigh," Tina called from somewhere up ahead in the crowd.

"I've got to go, Susan. Duty calls." She started after Tina then hesitated. Turning back, she added, "If you're not doing anything after school, Tina and I were going to get together at my house to listen to this new album she just bought. You're welcome to come too."

A troubled look crossed Susan's face, then she nodded. "Yeah, I'd like that," she smiled. "See you after school."

Leigh hurried to catch up with Tina.

"What's that all about?" Tina asked, glancing back at Susan.

"I invited her to come over later and listen to some music with us," Leigh answered. "Let's head back to my locker. I forgot my Social text."

Tina didn't say anything as they pushed through the still-busy hallway toward Leigh's locker to retrieve the book. She zigged, then zagged, artfully missing most of the kids they passed. "Susan was pretty cool at lunch, but it might be kind of risky inviting her over. I don't like the idea of dropping your shields when a Romulan War Bird has just decloaked."

Leigh ignored Tina's reference to her favourite sci-fi re-runs. "I just thought it was a good time to let bygones be bygones. We all have our own reasons for wanting the Falcons to win. As long as everybody ends up at the same place, the reasons don't matter."

Tina thought about this for a minute. "Okay," she agreed, "but just remember the 201st Rule of Acquisition."

Leigh sighed. Tina really was a MegaTrekkie. "And what might that be?"

"'Never consider a deal closed until you've spent their latinum," Tina quoted with authority as they arrived at Leigh's locker.

"What's that got to do with listening to music?" Leigh asked, confused.

"I just want you to remember she's Jimmy's sister," Tina said, as though that explained the whole conversation.

Not wanting to add to the confusion, Leigh nodded. "Okay, if you remember one thing also."

Tina looked at her. "Like what?"

"Like you've got to give someone a chance. If she screws up, fine, we can arm the photon torpedoes then. But until she does, I think we could spare a little friendship. After all, she's into hockey too," Leigh said, spinning the lock on the battered door.

"Nuh uh," Tina said shaking her head.

"Uh huh," Leigh retorted. The girls headed for class discussing whether Susan really liked hockey or was just into it because her brother was captain of the team, and whether she'd be so into it if her brother was the water boy instead.

★★★

Susan, Tina, and Leigh met outside after school and started for Leigh's house. The afternoon clouds were getting heavier and greyer. Leigh knew from the peculiar kind of light that it would snow soon.

She watched a small grey bird perching on a wire as Tina and Susan began chatting. The tiny bird was a ball of fluff and feathers as it tried to puff itself up to insulate against the falling temperatures. The thought of being a bird, free to fly anywhere, anytime with no rules had seemed so fantastic to Leigh last summer. Now, as she gave an involuntary shiver inside her warm jacket, she could see being free as a bird has its disadvantages, too. Today, she was glad to be herself with a warm house to go home to.

"Don't you think so?" Tina looked at her.

Leigh looked from Susan to Tina, confused. "I'm sorry, I guess I wasn't listening," she admitted, a little embarrassed.

Tina repeated her question. "Don't you think it's way tough?" She looked at Leigh's blank expression, sighed, and explained. "The new French teacher's habit of testing us on every little thing. Who cares if a car is masculine or feminine as long as it runs?" Tina sighed. "And I know they don't sound like Mrs. LeBlanc in Montreal, because my cousin was there this summer and their French isn't the same."

"My dad says the same thing," Susan volunteered. "It's like Quebec French is almost French, but not."

"Exactly," Tina said smiling warmly at Susan. "At last, someone who understands me," She grinned at Leigh.

Leigh grinned back. "I'll need a couple of years in therapy before I understand you, Kristina Blake."

Leigh thought about her own language lessons. During the weekends, she'd been learning to speak her mother's language on the reserve. She had to admit, when she tried to speak French it sounded chopped and awkward, but when she spoke Tsuu T'ina it was almost musical. In the Tsuu T'ina language, a couple of words turned into a whole picture.

She and her mother would translate some of the old stories and Leigh always thought about how many words it took in English to describe something, when one word in Tsuu T'ina said it all. Tina would think that was great. One of these days, Leigh would have to tell Tina about herself. However, today they had Susan along. Bad timing.

The girls turned in at Leigh's gate.

"I'll run home and get the best album ever," Tina said as she hurried toward her house. "Meet you in a minute."

Susan and Leigh continued up the snowy walk, their boots making a squeaky crunch as they went. "I'll get some hot chocolate on," Leigh called to Tina's retreating back.

Leigh unlocked the front door and pushed it open. She flipped on the inside light.

"You can hang your coat up in that closet," she told Susan as she kicked her boots off.

Susan hung up her coat as Leigh grabbed her pile of stuff and started for the kitchen. The light wasn't flashing on the answering machine, which was fine with Leigh, as she didn't want her company to hear any of the crank messages.

"I'll heat some milk in the microwave. Have a seat," she told Susan. She dumped her books on the kitchen table, then, looking at the stack, shoved them back behind the plant sitting in the middle.

Tina, who was as at home in Leigh's house as her own, came barging in the back door, CD in hand. Kicking off her boots, she tossed it on the table and immediately went to the fridge to check out the snack department.

"You've got to go shopping soon, Leigh. There's nothing to eat in your fridge," she complained, staring at the shelves of vegetables, fresh fruit, dairy products and leftover roast.

"I know, I told my dad, but he just laughed," Leigh said, reaching around Tina for the milk.

"We could make Rice Krispie squares if you have all the stuff," Susan offered.

"Hey, that's an idea. I love Rice Krispie squares. We make them ourselves about once a week." Leigh smiled at Susan. "I could check if we have marshmallows. What do you say, Tina? Are you up for it?"

Tina glanced at Susan, then shrugged her shoulders at Leigh.

"Whatever," she said unenthusiastically.

"Hey, you okay?" Leigh asked, noticing her friend's sudden mood change.

"Sure, I just thought RK's were something you and I did. I didn't know about the sudden truce with the Romulans."

"I'm not handing out defence codes. I just thought we could go to yellow alert instead of red," Leigh explained in a language Tina could understand.

Susan looked from Tina to Leigh, confused.

She was obviously a Twilighter, not a Trekkie. Leigh sighed and shrugged her shoulders. Sometimes Tina overreacted a little.

Tina went back to scanning the shelves for any sign of edible food.

Leigh made a beeline for the cupboard. She yanked

the door open and smiled at Susan. "So far so good," she said, tossing a bag of fluffy white marshmallows on the table.

Susan got up from the chair she'd been perched on and went to the fridge with Tina. "Any butter?" she asked.

"I don't know. I don't live here," Tina replied slamming the fridge door shut.

"There should be. Check that little compartment in the side of the door," Leigh said over her shoulder as she began rooting through another cupboard.

Tina slumped in a chair at the table while Susan located the butter and Leigh continued her search of the cupboard.

"Rats! I can't find the Rice Krispies. Did we use it all up last time?" she asked Tina.

"I can't remember," Tina said folding her arms and leaning back in her chair.

"All we've got is rolled oats and some kind of healthy bark and twig stuff my dad likes," Leigh said pulling the bag of oats out.

"Oh well, it was just an idea. No big deal," Susan said replacing the butter and closing the fridge door.

Tina sighed noisily and threw her arms up in the air. "I'd hate to be stranded on some Klingon outpost with you two. All we'd have to eat is *ro'qegh'Iwchab*!" she said, getting out of her chair and going to the cupboard.

Susan looked at Leigh, confused again.

"It's Klingon for 'rokeg blood pie' and you don't want to know what's in it," she explained, answering Susan's unasked question.

Tina proceeded to pull all manner of secret ingredients out of cupboards and drawers while issuing orders at the same time. "Saucepan, better get the big one out. That one, Susan," she said pointing to a drawer by the stove. "Leigh, we need that big bag of shredded coconut you bought when you were going to teach yourself to bake."

The kitchen became a flurry of activity.

"Chocolate, Leigh," Tina said, waving a spoon in the direction of the cupboard. "Sue, can you beat an egg and toss it in?"

"How about some of these maraschino cherries chopped up?" Susan asked, her head in the fridge in search of eggs.

"Great," Tina grinned at her. "Anything else looks appealing, bring it over."

Susan quickly mixed up a slurry of eggs with bits of red and green cherries floating in it. These she added to Tina's bubbling brew.

Leigh looked into the saucepan Tina was hovering over. The butter and chocolate had melted and Tina had added sugar, vanilla, coconut, and oats along with Susan's egg mixture. It looked pretty gross. Leigh reached into the pot and scooped a little out.

"It needs something crunchy, like…" she thought a minute, "chopped walnuts. I know where some are."

She ran to get the missing ingredient.

"Should I butter a pan to pour it into?" Susan asked Tina, who was busy trying to stir the thickening mixture.

Leigh arrived with the walnuts and promptly tossed them into the chocolate ooze.

"Good idea, Sue. I think this baby's done," Tina said, pulling the pan containing the brown sticky mess off the burner.

"I'd better get cracking on the hot chocolate or we won't have anything to wash that down with," Leigh said, grinning at Tina.

Susan began giggling. "It looks like we'll need something," she agreed as Tina squished the mixture into the greased pan Susan had prepared.

"I think it looks kind of like *qagh*," Tina said approvingly.

Susan looked at Leigh for a translation.

"'Serpent worm,' and I think it looks a lot better. This stuff's not moving." Leigh put their cups of chocolate into the microwave.

"Now this is what I call an after-school snack," Tina beamed as she sliced a generous portion of the congealed chocolate mixture for each of them.

"It's delicious, Tina. You'll have to give me the recipe," Susan giggled as she took a large bite.

"She's right, you outdid yourself this time, Tina. And it goes great with the hot chocolate," Leigh said, placing a cup in front of each of them.

"Mmmmmmph," Tina agreed, smiling at both Susan and Leigh while trying to chew an extremely large mouthful without any of the sticky chocolate mess escaping.

8 BAD TIMING

Tuesday came, and with it, the last hockey practice before the big game. It was going to be a tough one, Leigh knew, but the thought of the championship just days ahead made her want to practise even more.

She made her way home through the snowy streets. Tina had, of all things, a ballet lesson after school so Leigh was alone. She looked up at the solid layer of grey clouds. It was going to snow again. Real Canadian hockey weather, she thought with a smile.

Her house felt warm and safe as she slammed the front door. The light on the answering machine was busily blinking at her and Leigh hit the switch on her way by.

Her mom's soft voice spilled out of the machine, making Leigh feel better just hearing it.

"Hi, honey, how was school?" Her mom went on, "Your hair looks nice that way."

Leigh laughed as she carefully arranged her pickles on her peanut butter sandwich and continued to listen to her mom's message.

"Anyway, the reason I'm calling is to invite you to dinner tonight. I know this is out of the ordinary and rather short notice, Leigh, but there's something very important I want to discuss with you. I'll call your dad and explain things to him. I'll pick you up at 6:00 and we'll go grab a pizza. See you then, honey. I love you." The message ended.

Leigh stopped in mid-chew and stared at the machine. Dinner tonight! That was out of the question. It was the last practice before the big game. She had to go to this practice. She'd missed others because of juggling her schedule so both parents would be happy, but there was no way she could miss this one. No excuse would be good enough for Coach Stevenson tonight!

But her mom had sounded so excited and she never took Leigh out to supper on a weeknight. It had to be very important, but to whom? Her mom or to Leigh? Why did she have to call tonight?

Leigh had to do something, but what? Maybe if she called her mom and told her there was this majorly important exam tomorrow that the fate of the world would depend on…Her mom was a teacher, she could relate to that.

Leigh scrambled for the phone. Her mom might still be at school, she'd try there first. Leigh dialled the number to the elementary school on the reserve. It was the direct line to the staff room. Sometimes the teachers stayed late and they usually ended up drinking coffee in what the little kids called "The Bat Cave."

"Good afternoon, Trout Creek Elementary School. Mr. Two Feathers speaking."

Leigh took a deep breath. "Hello, Mr. Two Feathers. It's Leigh Aberdeen, is my mom still there? I need to talk to her, it's important." Leigh waited, crossing her fingers.

"Hi, Leigh. Gee, I'm not sure. Let me buzz her classroom and see if she's there."

Leigh could hear him using the intercom calling her mom's classroom. Unfortunately, she didn't hear anyone reply.

"Sorry, Leigh. Looks like she's left already."

Leigh sighed. "Thanks for trying, Mr. Two Feathers. Bye." Leigh hung up and quickly dialled her mom's home number. It was early. Her mom was sure to still be at home. Leigh listened as the phone rang in her ear.

Disappointedly, she heard the click of her mom's answering machine coming on. Maybe she was in the shower, "Mom, it's Leigh. If you're home, can you pick up or call me back? Thanks." Leigh waited, hoping, then hung up. Her fingers were getting cramped from being crossed so long.

There was one other thing she could do. If her mom hadn't yet called her dad to tell him about the evening's plans, perhaps she could convince her dad not to let her go. She could tell him about the big exam, then when he got home, say it had been cancelled and they were going to hockey practice instead. It was pretty lame, but she didn't have many options.

She dialled her dad's work number.

"Dad, it's me. Has mom called you yet?" she asked in a rush.

"Yes, she has and I told her there was no problem. In fact, since you'll be out with your mother, I'm planning on working late to try and finish this rush job I've been slaving over," he chuckled into the phone. "And Leigh, don't give your old dad a thought about not having any supper or lunch. I'll just make myself a baloney sandwich when I get home. Have a good time, honey."

"Sounds like you've got enough baloney to make that sandwich all right," she answered patiently. She said good-bye and slowly hung up the phone. Her mind ran over any other possible ways she could get out of this evening.

It looked like things were out of her hands. She'd run out of options.

There was only one thing left for Leigh to do. She would have to call the coach and try to explain her problem. She had to talk to him. This practice was going to be the most important one of the season.

They'd be going over strategy, plays, everything. Now she was going to miss it. This was not good.

Leigh looked up the coach's phone number and dialled. After four rings, his answering machine came on. Rats! She'd wanted to talk to him in person. Leigh took a deep breath and quickly explained to the machine how she couldn't make practice tonight, but could come over to have any tricky plays they'd be using Saturday explained to her. As she hung up the phone, she hoped she'd made sense.

She reluctantly went upstairs to change. One thing was for certain: she wasn't wearing any dumb dress.

★★★

At exactly six o'clock, her mom's old Toyota pulled up in the driveway. It looked strange sitting there. Leigh couldn't remember her mom ever coming here before.

She grabbed her coat and headed out.

"Hi, Mom," she said, slamming the car door shut after her. "This is really weird, dinner on a Tuesday night. Is everything okay?"

Her mom just smiled at her. "I'll tell you all about it when we get to the restaurant."

Leigh impatiently settled back for the drive.

The pizza parlour smelled great. Leigh's stomach growled as they waited to be seated. She watched as her boots made little puddles of melted snow while she stood beside her mom in line. They probably make you wait on purpose, she thought, until your boots are dry so you don't make a mess on their carpet. She'd decided since she couldn't get out of dinner with her mom, she'd make the best of it. After all, her mom didn't know about the practice, it wasn't her fault.

Finally, a smiling young lady ushered them into the dining room. They sat next to a crackling fire in a real stone fireplace, which made Leigh feel instantly better about the wait. She slipped off her coat and began scanning the menu. She'd never met a pizza she didn't like. In fact, she'd order the strangest combinations of toppings, just to try and find a gross one, but it never seemed to work. Once she'd ordered a Mexican special with added artichoke and tuna. It had been pretty tasty, especially with extra chili peppers.

Finally, they settled on a large super deluxe with extra anchovies, then Leigh looked over at her mom.

"So what s all the mystery about? You sounded really excited on the phone. It must be good news." She reached for a breadstick as she waited for her mom to answer.

Her mom smiled at her. "You could say I'm excited. I think you will be too when you hear what's happening." She clasped her hands in front of her and began. "There's going to be an important recital and Wind Dancer's going to participate." She looked at Leigh, who was waiting for her mom to explain what this had to do with her. "The recital will be televised and with all the added exposure, Wind Dancer stands a good chance of being invited to the Canadian Traditional Dance Finals in Toronto. If we win, that could mean a world tour this summer, and a big financial boost for the troupe."

"Gee, mom, that is cool. But…" She was just going

to ask her mom how she fit into the picture when her mom held up her hand and stopped her.

"I haven't finished telling you the exciting part. I discussed your progress with the other members of the group and we all think you're ready to join us. We've created a special segment where the central figure is a Fancy Dancer—you," she smiled at Leigh. "And the other members with you complement your dance, but are separate from it. We tried it out at rehearsal and it works. I think it's a fantastic opportunity for all of us. What do you say?" She reached for a breadstick.

Leigh sat dumbfounded. Finally, she found her voice. "Wow! That is awesome! Do you really think I'm ready? Oh Mom, I could wear my new dress and I have this ace routine where I use all the steps you taught me and a couple I thought up myself." She was getting excited now. This was something she hadn't expected.

Her mom was speaking again. "When you come over Friday, we can go over the entrance and exit and where you'll be in relation to the other dancers. You should try on your new dress so I can make any alterations before Saturday, and if you need anything we'll have time to get it."

"Wait a minute," Leigh said, her mind racing. "What did you just say?"

"I said we, or I guess me since I'll be the one doing last-minute errands, would have time to pick up any extra things you need before Saturday." She smiled at her daughter.

Leigh felt like she'd turned to stone. "Saturday? The dance recital is this Saturday? When this Saturday?"

"Why, at 4:00 at the Theatre for the Performing Arts." She smiled at Leigh. "You're not nervous, are you, honey? Because you needn't be. I've been watching you and you're great. You have a natural athletic ability which comes out in your dance. You really are a good dancer."

Leigh couldn't breathe. Saturday—the most important Saturday in her hockey life and her mom springs this on her. She had to think. The timing was unbelievable. The championship game started at 3:00. There was no way she could play hockey and make the dance recital at 4:00! It was impossible to be in two places at once even if you wanted to be—and she did. Hockey and dancing were the two things in life that really mattered to her. All the other Saturdays in the world and it had to be hers that got screwed up.

She smiled weakly at her mom. "I think this is really great, Mom," she said lamely.

Just then, their pizza came and Leigh busied herself eating.

She still had a few days. But how could she solve the growing mountain of problems she had before then?

9 CUT!

"How was your dinner with your mom?" Tina asked as they took off their coats at Leigh's house.

Tina did a pirouette across the kitchen floor to the fridge. She was Leigh's best friend, and Leigh thought she was the greatest, but when she did that ballet stuff, she looked really dumb. Tina said she took ballet to "round out her social graces." Leigh watched her do a plié. She looked like a fat lady trying to pick up a dime.

"Dinner was great, it was the timing that sucked," Leigh said shaking her head. "There are way too many things happening right now, Tina. I don't know how I'm going to pull this one off."

"What do you mean?" Tina asked, confused as she flopped very un-ballerina-like into a chair.

Leigh realized she'd said too much. Now was not the time to try to explain her life story. Maybe after the weekend when things weren't so scrambled.

"Oh, you know, school, the big game on Saturday, my hair...stuff, just too much stuff." "Stuff" was an explanation Tina could understand.

Tina wriggled in her chair. "I know what you mean. My own hair's been driving me nuts lately."

Leigh headed to the fridge and surveyed the contents. She pulled the box of leftover pizza out of the fridge. She loved cold pizza. It made the perfect after-school snack.

Tina grinned when she saw the box. "Cool, real food!" Then she noticed the flashing light on the answering machine. "Hey, you've got a message on your machine. Want me to play it?" she asked and before Leigh could stop her, she pushed the play button.

Leigh cringed. What if it was her mom with more news about the native dance recital?

Coach Stevenson's voice filled the room.

"...and since you were unable to attend last night's practice, which tells me you've obviously got some problems with hockey and where it stands on your list of priorities, I'm afraid I'm going to have to replace you in the lineup on Saturday. I've overlooked your missed practices before, but this time we need to play as a team—a real team, with all players giving a hundred percent to the Falcons. I just don't think you have the right team spirit or willingness to follow the rules."

The message ended. Both Leigh and Tina stared at the answering machine. This was unbelievable.

Leigh started shaking her head. She wanted to say something, but no words would come out. Not play on

Saturday? There had to be a mistake. Of course she'd play on Saturday—she had to! It was the first step in her Big Plan. Her dream was to play for the Calgary Flames, and now it was in serious jeopardy. Hockey was something she really wanted, but now it seemed she might not get the chance. She shuddered.

"This stinks," Tina said in her usual way of cutting to the heart of things.

"I can't believe it. I've worked hard for my place on the Falcons. I deserve to be there Saturday." Leigh sat down next to Tina. "The coach says I don't have team spirit. That's not true! I have so much spirit, I practically breathe hockey. You know Tina, I even thought of this real cool play we could use. It takes three men and a lot of team play, but it's practically a sure goal scorer. I have it all worked out in my head. One man takes the faceoff, passes it to a teammate who's already down ice, who in turn passes it to another player, who follows the puck across the blue line and slams it home before the other team can figure out what we're doing. It will work, if I just get the chance to play."

Leigh's mind was going around in circles. She'd have to talk to the coach, in person, and as soon as possible.

★★★

All through school the next day she thought about what she could do. There were few options. Her one chance was to go to the arena after school, pray the coach was there, and try to explain things to him.

"I'm not going straight home today. I've got something to do first," she explained to Tina as they headed outside after last class.

"Yeah, what?" Tina asked.

"I'm going over to the arena and see if Coach Stevenson is there," Leigh said. "But you don't have to come. I'll just call you later and tell you how it went."

"Like I'm not going with you. As if that's even a possibility," Tina said, pulling the collar up on her coat. "Who'll arm the photon torpedoes if you need them? Who'll make sure your shields are working?"

"Good point," Leigh said, grinning at her friend as they both headed to the arena.

When they arrived, they were met by a stern-looking security guard.

"Hi. I'm Leigh Aberdeen and I'm looking for Coach Stevenson. I play on the Falcons and I need to talk to him," Leigh explained. "Is he here?"

The guard looked at her skeptically. "I thought the Falcons were a boys' team. You sure you play on the team and not your brother?" the guard asked.

Tina rolled her eyes and Leigh shot her a silencing look. "I know it's strange. I'm the only girl on the team. The coach will verify that if you call him."

The guard mumbled something about new-fangled feminist ideas as he dialled an internal extension on the phone. Leigh held her breath. What if he wasn't here, or worse yet, what if he wouldn't speak to her and let her explain?

The surly guard hung up the phone. "He says to go in. He's in the boys' dressing room."

Leigh nodded to the guard, while Tina grinned like a Cheshire cat as they headed into the building to find the coach.

Leigh stepped into the entranceway of the dressing room and took off her toque and mitts. She tried to think of something brilliant to say to convince the coach to let her play. All she could think of was the fact she was a fast skater and knew all the plays. Lame.

He glanced up as she came into the room. Leigh looked at the stack of extra equipment he was sorting out. Spares for Saturday in case someone broke a stick or needed tape.

"Hello, Leigh. You must be here because of the message I left on your machine. I'm afraid I'm going to have to stand by my decision. It wasn't an easy one, but I have to think of the entire team, not just one player." He went back to the sticks.

Leigh didn't know what to say. She just stood in the doorway. Tina, who was quietly standing behind her, suddenly reached out and gave her a little shove. Leigh was propelled into the room at high speed.

"Hey!" she blurted out, then regaining control of her balance, stopped her headlong entry. "I mean, excuse me

Coach, but this is really important to me and I need to talk to you about it. I'm clear on the message, but I don't understand why you want to cut me. I called you about the dinner with my mother and I tried to explain I absolutely, positively couldn't get out of it."

The coach held up his hand. "Leigh, we've been through this before. Sure you're a fine hockey player, but that's only part of it. Practices are part of the discipline involved with playing on a team. You've missed a lot of practices over the past couple of months and your excuses are getting pretty thin." He shook his head. "Perhaps hockey's not the game for you. There are lots of other sports, like tennis, that rely solely on your ability alone. They might be more what you're looking for."

Leigh felt the first stirrings of panic. "Coach, I was born to play hockey, and I want to play for the Falcons. I understand why you're ticked at me for missing practices and the effect it has on team spirit and morale. But I honestly do put hockey first. If you knew what I go through just so I can play, you'd know how much it means to me. I just have trouble juggling my hockey schedule with the stuff my folks have planned. If you'll let me play this one game, I promise I'll figure something out so this doesn't happen again."

She held her breath as she waited…and waited. Finally the coach slowly nodded his head.

"Okay Leigh, you have a deal. But this is your last

chance. I have to answer to the parents of the other players. There has to be only one set of rules for all the players and that includes you." He went back to checking the equipment.

Leigh turned to leave, grinning at Tina as she passed her. She wanted to get out of there before he had a chance to change his mind again. She didn't think she could handle any more stress today.

★★★

Leigh had felt so good after meeting with the coach, she'd completely forgotten about her other problem. The dance recital. She thought about it as she got ready for bed.

The moon was full and the pale light made crazy shadows across her walls as she lay thinking. She'd always thought the shapes looked like hockey players streaking around her room as she waited for sleep, but tonight, they seemed like black, creepy ghosts.

There was no way she was going to be able to go to the dance recital. She wasn't even sure how she was going to get out of going to her mom's on the weekend as it was, but to tell her mom she couldn't go to the dance recital because she had to play hockey was out of the question. No, it just wasn't going to happen. Leigh thought about explaining to the team why she couldn't go out for the planned season wind-up supper after the game because she had to go find out how her Native mother's dance group did at the recital she was supposed to have performed in! Oh yeah, that would be good. Even Tina would wonder about her.

The only thing to do was convince her mom she couldn't dance. Maybe a sudden attack of the clumsies, or perhaps some kind of accident. Leigh felt her eyes start to sting with tears. She'd really wanted to dance, but there was just no way it could happen. And besides, there'd be other dance recitals. Her mom had said she was a good dancer; she'd just have to postpone her dancing debut for another time.

Leigh rolled over and squeezed her eyes shut. Tomorrow was Friday. After school, she'd go to her mom's for the start of their big weekend.

10 TAKING A DIVE

Her mom was at the meeting hall rehearsing with Wind Dancer when Leigh's dad dropped her off the next day. He always drove Leigh out to the reserve so her mom didn't have to come to their house to pick her up. He would also come to the reserve to get her on Sunday evening. This weekend would be different, however. Leigh's dad would pick her up after lunch on Saturday and take her to the game. She'd prearranged that with no problem.

She'd tell her mom she was going to a surprise birthday slumber party for Tina Saturday night and would be back Sunday. Then she'd be able to play in the big game and go to the banquet after with no problems. A great plan—before the whole dance recital thing had come up.

Now she'd have to do something a lot more extreme if she were going to get out of the recital without explaining everything to everyone. She was really sorry she'd have to miss it, but this was the Championship.

"Hi, honey," her mother called to her as Leigh pulled off her coat and boots. Leigh could feel the rhythmic beat of the drum music through the stockinged soles of her feet.

She moved over beside her mom and watched as the dancers whirled and moved gracefully to the music. Her mom smiled down at her, then continued watching the dancers.

Finally the music ended and the group broke up for a rest before starting the next number.

"I'm so excited, Leigh. Wait till you see how your dress turned out." She led Leigh over to a table.

"What do you think?" her mom asked as Leigh stared.

It was the most beautiful Fancy dress she'd ever seen. The bright colours shimmered and the beadwork was extraordinary. The full skirt was sewn so the intricately arranged reds and oranges flowed into one another in a kaleidoscope of colour.

The different panels were accented with thin tracings of black which made the design stand out vividly. There was also a perfectly matched headdress with feathers the exact colours of the dress and it was held together with tiny bells which would tinkle as she danced.

But the thing that really took Leigh's breath away was the matching shawl. Her mother had crafted the design out of the same colours, but when Leigh was wearing the shawl and spread her arms, the hidden design was revealed. It was a large, luminous butterfly with outstretched wings. "Oh, Mom," Leigh whispered.

"Turned out rather well, don't you think?" her mom asked, smiling.

"Mom, this is the coolest dress I've ever seen. It's so, so…" Leigh searched for the right word. "Awesome!"

"Well, I'm just glad you like it," her mom said, pleased with Leigh's reaction. "You'll look 'awesome' wearing it tomorrow night."

Leigh felt her stomach tighten. How could she tell her mom she wasn't going to dance tomorrow? It made her feel sick.

"Would you like to try the routine we've come up with for your big night?" her mom was asking.

Leigh tried to smile at her mom. "Sure, sounds great."

Leigh went through the staging with the other dancers. Finally, they were ready to begin a full rehearsal. The drums started softly, then built as the dancers began the routine.

Leigh told herself she had no choice. She loved hockey. Tomorrow was the biggest game of her life. She started dancing. As the music grew louder and faster, Leigh began a series of intricate steps which would lead to the finale. She stole a quick look at her mom's smiling face, then closing her eyes, she stepped sideways, cried out in pain, and fell to the floor.

The drums immediately stopped as everyone crowded around Leigh. She grabbed her ankle and began moaning.

"It hurts really bad," she said to her mother, whose worried face was tight with anxiety.

The other dancers helped Leigh to a chair. Leigh continued to show great amounts of pain.

Her mother picked up Leigh's foot and gingerly moved her ankle.

"Ow, I think it's sprained," Leigh said, trying to make herself cry for good measure.

"It's not broken," her mom said, carefully placing the foot on a neighbouring chair. "This is terrible. Maybe we'd best get you to a doctor." Her mom looked anxiously at Leigh.

Leigh thought quickly. "Mom, tomorrow is Wind Dancer's big chance. I don't think I'll be able to dance and I don't want you to have to babysit me. Maybe we should call Dad to come and pick me up so I can rest at my house. That way I won't feel worse by keeping you from rehearsing."

She saw her mom hesitating.

Leigh added hurriedly, "I'll put ice on it and if it still hurts tomorrow, I'll go to the clinic and get it checked out by a doctor." She looked up at her mom.

"I don't know, Leigh." Her mom was shaking her head now.

"Look, I'm sure it's just a bad sprain. You said yourself it's not broken. I just need to rest it." Leigh waited.

"Okay," her mom said with a sigh, "maybe that's best. Your father can keep a close eye on you." Her brow furrowed. "This is the worst luck, honey, but don't worry. There'll be other chances to dance." She smiled worriedly at Leigh. "And your dress will still be here."

Leigh felt awful. "I guess you're right, Mom. I was really looking forward to the recital," she smiled at her mom, "especially after I saw that awesome dress."

Somehow, she'd have to make this up to her mom, Leigh promised herself as she waited for her dad to pick her up. She wished things could be different.

★★★

All the way home, Leigh felt worse than if she really had sprained her ankle. She hated lying to her mom, but what choice did she have?

Her dad had been surprised by the call and even more surprised when Leigh had told him about her injury.

"Gee, sweetie, do you think you'll have to miss the game tomorrow?" her dad asked as Leigh explained about the ankle.

"No, I think I just twisted it wrong. I'll go to bed and rest it, then call Mom tomorrow morning and tell her how it is. That way she won't worry," Leigh had volunteered as they drove home.

"That's a good idea, Leigh," her dad agreed.

Her dad helped her to her room and applied an ice pack to her sprained ankle.

"It doesn't look swollen, Leigh, but keep the ice on

it for a while just to be sure," he'd said as he pulled her door closed. "Call me if you need anything. I'll be right downstairs." He smiled at her.

"Don't worry, Dad. I'm sure I'll be fine tomorrow."

I may never be fine again, Leigh thought as she tossed the ice pack onto the chair in the corner. She lay back on her pillow, but it was hard to go to sleep.

11 DIRTY PLAY

Saturday morning Leigh awoke early. She wanted to call her mom before her dad woke, in case he listened in on her conversation. She wasn't a very good liar, and it was going to be tough enough without having to explain her lies to her dad.

She dialled her mom's number and waited.

"Hello," her mom's soft voice responded.

"Hi, Mom, it's me," Leigh said, trying to sound normal.

"How's the ankle, honey?" her mom asked, the concern immediately obvious in her voice.

"It's still pretty sore," Leigh lied, "but I'm keeping ice packs on it and the swelling seems to be going down. I think if I stay off it today, it should be better by tomorrow." She hoped her mom's years as a teacher wouldn't alert her to Leigh's made-up story.

"I still think you should go to a doctor," her mom said firmly. "You never know, even a simple sprain can have complications."

Leigh thought of her mom's bad leg and knew why

she was reacting this way. "I'm keeping a close eye on it, Mom, and so is Dad. Don't worry, if anything weird shows up, we'll go right to the doctor's." She tried to change the subject. "Hey, good luck tonight. I'll be thinking of you as I watch it on TV." Leigh decided she'd have to record the program so she could watch the performance after they got home from the banquet. That way, when she phoned her mom on Sunday morning, she'd know just what to say. This lying business was getting really complicated. She just hoped nothing went wrong.

"I'll be thinking of you too, honey." Her mom's voice sounded sad. "But we'll have other dance recitals and you're only going to get better with your dancing. I'm sure of that. Call me tomorrow and we'll talk. Take care of that foot. I love you. Bye."

Leigh felt crummy as she hung up on her mother.

"Was that your mom?" her dad asked as he joined her in the kitchen.

"Yes, I was just calling to tell her my foot feels great. All it needed was a good night's rest and I'm ready to play hockey." She smiled up at her dad.

"You're sure you're up to the game?" he asked searching her face. "You're not just saying that because it's the championship and you don't want to let the team down?"

Leigh swallowed hard. "My ankle's great, Dad, honest. I feel like I could skate forever." She went to get a cereal bowl as her dad began making coffee. This was hard, but she only had to keep it together until tonight

★★★

They headed down to the rink just after lunch. Leigh had eaten lots, knowing she always got hungry halfway through a game. This was one time she didn't want to be distracted by her stomach complaining it wanted more food.

"Why don't you drop your gear off in the dressing room, and come meet some of my friends," Leigh's dad had suggested as they entered the arena.

"Sure, Dad," Leigh said, heading for one of the women's washrooms which had been set aside for players' use. "I'll be back in a minute." She noticed several other Falcon players already suited up and doing some warm-up drills.

She didn't see Jimmy, but Susan was sitting in the stands with her parents, so Leigh figured he must already be here. She wondered if the others had heard of the coach's plan to cut her from the team, and if they had, whether they knew he'd changed his mind. No sense wondering, she'd know soon enough.

Tossing her bulky equipment bag into the washroom, Leigh headed back to meet her dad. As she started up the stairs, she saw Jimmy standing at the top, looking down at her.

"What are you doing here, Aberdeen? Didn't you get the word? The Falcons are an all-boys' team again, just like they should be. No girls allowed." His arms were folded; the expression on his face was satisfied.

"Gee Jimmy, didn't you hear? That kind of thinking is not only against the law, it's stupid."

Jimmy angrily headed down the stairs and shoved his way past her, deliberately bumping her into the wall in the process.

"Consider that your first check of the game, Aberdeen," he snarled at her. "I'm going to find Coach Stevenson and let him know you're here. We'll see if you should be down here with us, or up in the stands with the fans."

Leigh watched him storm down the passageway. At least she had her answer; the coach was going to spring her on the guys. Leigh was sure a lot of the players would welcome her, especially when it was the Devon Dynamos they were facing. They would need all the aces they could get in their hand.

Meeting her dad's friends made Leigh feel strange. Her dad was always so proud of her, but today he made a real fuss about her being the only girl on the team and how well she played. He told them how Leigh could hold her own in a check and could out-skate most of the boys out there. Leigh smiled and nodded awkwardly, then excused herself and headed back down to get changed. Having a finger pointed at you because you're different is always hard, but when it's your own dad doing the pointing, it really made a girl feel uncomfortable.

The arena was starting to fill. It was going to be a packed house.

Leigh went to the women's washroom where she had left her equipment and began dressing. She took extra care, making sure everything was on just right and as comfortably as possible. For this game, she wanted to be at her best. She hoped to get a skate in with the guys before the game, just so everyone was cool with her on the ice. Jimmy had a way of convincing people things should be the way he wanted them to be. However, she'd let her skating do her convincing. When it came right down to it, the guys would let action speak louder than words. This was hockey.

Suddenly, she stopped and looked around. Her skates were nowhere to be seen. She knew she'd brought them in with her, she'd packed them herself. Panic grabbed at her. No skates, no game.

There was only one explanation. Someone had taken them. Leigh headed for the guys' dressing room.

She pounded on the door. Robert's head appeared a minute later. "Can I come in?" she demanded. Robert stood aside to let her pass.

Leigh burst into the dressing room. She was so angry, her voice shook when she spoke.

"Okay, Jimmy, what did you do with them?" she demanded, trying not to shout.

Everyone stopped talking and turned to look at her.

Jimmy grinned maliciously. "Well, well, if it isn't little Leigh Aberdeen. You may have whined to the coach so he'd let you back on the team, but the guys have decided not to let you play today. We don't want you. Am I right, guys?"

Trevor and Michael noisily agreed with Jimmy and a couple of others half-heartedly nodded, but the rest of the team said nothing.

"Go sit in the stands with the other wannabes. The Falcons have a championship to win," he said dismissively.

Leigh's temper flared. "Don't hand me that garbage, Jimmy. I asked you where my skates are. Now tell me what you've done with them." She looked over at his equipment bag which lay open on the floor.

Jimmy saw where she was looking and stepped in front of her to block her view. "Keep away from my gear, Aberdeen, or I might chase you with my jock strap." He sniggered at her.

"Look, I don't want any trouble from you, Jimmy. I just want my skates back." She tried to keep her voice down.

"You don't have a spare pair with you?" he asked sarcastically, then added with a snort, "I guess you'll have to go to the store and buy yourself some figure skates like all the other girls."

"I've had about all I'm going to take from you. I've

put up with the threatening answering machine messages and the nasty notes left on my locker at school, but this is the final straw. I want my skates and I want them now," she demanded, her voice deadly calm.

Jimmy seemed momentarily confused. "Wait a minute, I don't know what you're talking about. What messages and notes? You've got a real problem, Aberdeen." He shook his head.

"Don't deny it. I know you've been behind these rotten tactics from the start. When the thug phone messages telling me to quit the Falcons or else weren't enough, you stuck nasty notes to my locker telling me again to quit. And when those weren't enough, you tried to make it so tough for me out on the ice that I'd stop playing for my own health." She stared at him, daring him to deny it again after she'd spelled it out so clearly.

"C'mon, Jimmy," Robert said slamming the door on his locker. "Enough is enough. Give Leigh back her skates."

Leigh looked around the room at the other players.

"Yeah, Jimmy, we've got a game to win," someone added.

Leigh looked at the player who'd said this. It was Trevor Greene.

Jimmy glared at Leigh, then grudgingly went to his equipment bag and retrieved her skates.

"Here," he said, tossing them at Leigh's feet. "Now leave."

Leigh picked up her skates and retreated from the dressing room.

12 THE WINNING PLAY

Leigh had never skated so fast or pushed herself so hard before in her life. Despite everyone's super efforts, the Falcons were still down one by a score of 4–3. The Dynamos were playing better and meaner than ever. There had already been two Falcon players sent to the dressing room because of monster heavy checks. It hadn't stopped the Falcons. Each player knew what it would take to win and everyone was giving a hundred and ten percent.

The whistle blew and adrenalin had Leigh moving before she even realized she'd managed to grab the puck on the faceoff. She dodged around a Dynamo and pushed her legs to take her further into enemy territory. She already had one goal to her credit in the game, but, she smiled to herself, she wouldn't mind two.

Jimmy cut in front of her and for one split second, Leigh thought he was going to make a run at her for the puck. Instead, he viciously checked the Dynamo defenceman who'd been coming up on her left to blindside her.

She cut right and scanned down ice for a familiar face. She could see Robert moving into position in the slot. If she could take the puck behind the net, then pass it out to him instead of trying the expected wraparound, they stood a good chance of catching the goalie off guard. Leigh pushed a little harder.

She was really sailing as she cut around behind the net. Robert was moving into position. Suddenly, out of the corner of her eye, Leigh saw a big Dynamo defenceman ram into Robert from behind. Robert went down hard.

Leigh had no choice. She was committed. Pulling her stick with the puck in close to her, she cut hard at the edge of the net as she came out from behind and flipped the puck up off the ice and into the far corner of the goal. The goalie had been positioned for a low, tight shot and the puck skimmed over his shoulder as it sunk home.

The red light began whirling, signifying a clean goal. The Falcon fans were on their feet cheering. Leigh couldn't help doing a little victory dance on skates as she moved to the Falcon bench. Everyone patted the top of her helmet as she sat recovering from her very successful shift.

She felt great. The game was tied 4–4 and she'd scored her second goal. All they had to do now was get one more goal in the remaining time and the championship was theirs. One more goal—if you said it fast enough, it didn't sound that tough to get. Leigh looked over at the Dynamo bench.

Their players seemed so big. In fact, nearly all their players were in their last year in Peewee. Next year, the Dynamos would have a team of mostly young, small players. With a team like that, they probably wouldn't make the championship.

That might be part of the reason they were playing so brutally hard. It was the older guys' last chance to win before going on to Bantam where they would be the rookies, and it was the younger guys' only shot before their odds went way down with next year's new, inexperienced players. Leigh could understand their reasons for playing the way they had been.

The tension was electric in the arena. Everyone knew what was riding on the next goal. Coach Stevenson was using his big guns more and more each shift, but it wasn't doing any good. That winning goal eluded both teams. Everyone watched as the clock counted down the final minutes in the game, 3-2-1—the horn sounded and the Falcons were into overtime.

Both sides had a short rest period before starting the sudden death period. All the players on both teams had given their all, but it hadn't been enough. Now they would be asked to give more. Leigh followed the rest of the team to the dressing room for their last strategy meeting. Coach Stevenson would need to pull a big rabbit out of his hat. The Falcons were tired. Michael and Robert sat slumped against their lockers. Their helmets were off and their hair was plastered to their heads with sweat. Other players were wiping their faces with wet towels or sucking down fruit juices like they'd just been rescued from a desert island. Jimmy looked exhausted as he poured water over his face. Skating against the bigger, stronger Dynamo players had taken its toll.

"I know you guys have really worked your butts off and I'm proud of you. I want you to remember that. Win or lose, you've made the name 'Falcons' one the Dynamos will never forget." He smiled as he spoke to the assembled players.

"However, it's not over yet. We have one more goal to score…" Coach Stevenson looked around the room at the exhausted faces looking to him for a miracle. "You're tired, I know, I can see it. You deserve to be, you've really kept those Dynamo hacks skating, but I want you to shake it off. I want you to go back out there like it was the opening of the game and you're ready to take them down." He paused and folded his arms before he continued. "Look at it this way: if you get one more goal, I promise I'll let you take your skates off until September." This got a lot of smiles from the kids and everyone felt better knowing the coach appreciated how hard they'd tried.

The team filed back upstairs to finish off the Dynamos.

★★★

The overtime period began with a bang as two opposing players started scrapping right after the opening faceoff. Tempers were running high and the Dynamos were famous for their quick use of muscle. Leigh made sure she was extra careful to stay out of any Dynamos' way. As the only girl, she'd always been an obvious target for checks. Fortunately, years of being the obvious target had honed her dodging skills on skates. With her speed, she was a hard target to hit.

The period dragged on with neither side claiming victory. This had to be the longest championship game in history.

Leigh was just coming in from a gruelling shift, when she spotted Jimmy talking to Coach Stevenson. Immediately following, the coach called for a time out.

"Jimmy's come up with a new play that's going to win this game for us…" the coach began as he called his team into a quick strategy session.

Much to Leigh's surprise, he then went on to explain her three-man play to everyone. Leigh looked at Jimmy, but he avoided her eyes.

"Okay, Jimmy, you and Robert will set up the play and Leigh, I want you to take it home. Any questions?" he asked.

"But Coach," Jimmy protested, "since it's my play, I think I should be the shooter, not Leigh."

"I know you'd like to go out in a blaze of glory, Jimmy, but I need you for muscle and Robert to stickhandle or we won't get a chance to score. Besides, Leigh is small, fast, and good in close. She's the best skater for a play like this. Trevor, you're the best man to take the faceoff. You'll play centre for this play. Okay, let's go," he said, pre-empting Jimmy's next argument.

Robert winked at her as they went over the boards and set up for the faceoff.

Leigh smiled back. "Remember, Rob, take no prisoners." He grinned and headed to centre ice. Leigh had been so surprised the coach was going to use her play, she never had time to confront Jimmy with the fact he'd stolen it from her. He skated past her and took up his position to start the three-man play.

The Dynamos knew something was up, and each player was covering his man even closer than before. Jimmy, however, was big enough to muscle his way past any guard. All they had to do to start the play was get control of the puck from the faceoff.

Leigh looked at Trevor. Everything depended on his winning the faceoff. He glanced at Leigh. She nodded to him and grinned. He relaxed and grinned back.

The puck seemed to drop in slow motion as Leigh watched it fall from the ref's hand. It took forever to hit the ice.

The instant it touched, Trevor was on it, tipping it to Jimmy. Leigh didn't wait to see what happened next. She had to get down ice to the blue line before anyone had a chance to cover her. The play depended on speed and catching the Dynamos off guard. There was no setting up.

Jimmy spun and passed it to Robert who was waiting at the far side of the rink right on the blue line. Timing was crucial. Robert smoothly guided the puck into position and shot it past the blue line into Dynamo territory.

The instant Leigh saw Robert fire the puck, she was across the blue line and skating deep into Dynamo ice after the puck. Her legs burned from the force of the exertion after an already hard game, but she ignored the pain as she came up on the puck.

The speed of the puck had slowed since Robert had launched it, but it was still going at a good clip. Leigh had to time her stroke just perfectly so she could use the forward motion of the puck to simply accelerate it into the goal.

She could hear her breath rasp in her throat, but there was no time to ease the burning in her lungs. She pulled her stick back, glanced at the Dynamo goal, not even seeing the goalie, and refocused on the puck.

She felt her stick connect and the sound it made was that wonderful hard thwack of the puck hitting the sweet spot at precisely the right place.

The puck blasted from her stick like it had exploded from a gun. It went down ice faster than any shot she'd ever made.

The goalie never had a chance. He tried to spread

himself to cover as much of the net as possible, but nothing could stop Leigh's shot.

The red light began whirling the victory signal as the arena exploded in a frenzy of cheering. Horns blew, whistles shrilled, and everywhere, fans from both teams were on their feet cheering the slickest play of the game.

Leigh skated past the dejected Dynamo goalie.

"Good game," she called good-naturedly. He waved his stick tiredly in her direction and slowly skated toward his bench.

Leigh stopped midway back to her bench. It suddenly hit her. She had scored her third goal of the game—a hat trick, her first hat trick ever. Life was sweet. If she ever had grandchildren, she already had her favourite story to tell them.

The players on the bench spilled over the boards surrounding Jimmy, Robert, and Leigh as the proud trio skated up to the jubilant group.

From somewhere, Leigh tried to remember to be a gracious winner as both teams lined up to congratulate each other on a battle well fought. But all the while, her face was plastered with the biggest smile any twelve-year-old had ever had.

★★★

The dressing room was pandemonium. Everywhere, players were congratulating each other for feats beyond any kid's imaginings. Leigh joined in the celebration. There was no question of her not being there because she was a girl on a boys' team. At this moment, she was simply one of the best darn hockey players the Falcons had ever had.

She let herself be carried away in the rush of emotions that filled the dressing room. As she laughed and acknowledged the other players' contributions in a mutual exchange of glowing praise, her dad and Tina materialized at her side.

"*Qapla!*" Tina gleefully shouted.

"Success!" Leigh agreed.

Her dad gave her a hug. "Wonderful game, honey. I'm so proud of you. Did you hear me cheering you on? I know I won't be able to talk tomorrow from all the shouting. I'm so proud of you." Leigh had never heard her dad so excited. He was positively elated.

"Well Dad, you know it was a full team effort," Leigh said, a little embarrassed at her father's obvious pride in his little girl.

"Well, I'm going to be the happiest dad at the victory banquet tonight when my little girl gets voted most valuable player in the championship." Her father beamed. "If it's okay with you, a few of my friends are coming back to our place to celebrate the Falcons' win with us. While you have a bubble bath or whatever young ladies do before banquets, we guys will rehash the game and your winning goal."

Leigh noticed Coach Stevenson motioning for her to join him. She excused herself and followed the coach over to a corner away from the rest of the crowd.

"What's up, Coach?" she asked.

"It's been brought to my attention by a reliable source that the three-man play we used wasn't Jimmy's at all, but yours. Is this true?" He looked stern.

Leigh caught a glimpse of Tina, a 1000-watt grin plastered to her face, watching them.

It wasn't hard to figure out who the "reliable source" was. Leigh shuffled her feet, wishing she'd taken her skates off. "Well, actually, yeah, I guess it was." She felt like she was in trouble.

"Why didn't you say something?" Coach Stevenson asked, puzzled.

"Because it didn't matter where the play came from, as long as it worked and the Falcons won. Anyway, Jimmy knew it was my play." She glanced across the room at Jimmy, who was also keeping an eye on her and the coach. "Besides," she added, blushing, "I stole it from the Calgary Flames in the first place and just changed it a little to fit our team."

"I owe you an apology, Leigh. You're not the one who needs to be reminded about team spirit. In fact, I think the Falcons are a lucky team to have a player like you with them." He smiled at her. "And I don't think you should be too surprised if you're wearing a 'C' on your uniform next year."

Leigh beamed up at the coach. "Cool!" was all she could manage.

Everyone was still yelling and laughing as they patted each other on the back and punched each other good-naturedly. The Forest Park Falcons were winners, all of them, and everyone was celebrating.

Contentedly, Leigh sat enjoying the good mood in the room, when she happened to glance over to the door.

There, framed in the doorway, was her mother. She was dressed in full costume for the dance recital tonight, complete with beads, buckskin, and feathers. Leigh took a deep gulp of air.

13 MOCCASINS AND SKATES

Leigh jumped up from the bench she'd been perched on. Pushing her way through the boisterous crowd, she grabbed her mother's arm and quickly ushered her out into the deserted hall.

"Mom, what are you doing here?" she asked, knowing she sounded guilty and out of excuses.

Her mother clasped her hands tightly together in front of her like she always did when she was very upset or angry. When she spoke, her voice was low and controlled.

"When we arrived at the recital, we were told we wouldn't be performing until near the end of the show—about two hours into the program. That meant I would have time to go see my daughter who was too injured to dance with us before we went on."

Her face was stony as she continued. "However, when I arrived at my daughter's house, I was told by the neighbours that the Aberdeens were at a hockey tournament until later. Imagine my surprise when I hurried to the arena in time to see my daughter score the winning goal for her hockey team." Her voice sounded more hurt than angry now. Leigh would have found anger easier to deal with.

"Mom, I can explain," she began like every guilty kid had begun since the dawn of time. She glanced furtively around to see if anyone had noticed her leaving with the Indian woman. They were alone in the dimly lit corridor.

"You don't have to make up lies for me, Leigh," her mother said in a voice Leigh had never heard before. "I'm sorry you feel ashamed of your people, Leigh, and they are *your* people. I understand how hard it is for you living with your father and knowing the way he feels, but you've got to make up your own mind about who and what you are. That's one decision no one can make for you."

She turned to go, then stopped. "I love you, Leigh. You are my daughter," she smiled ruefully. "My hockey-star daughter."

Leigh watched as her mother walked quickly up the passageway to the dark stairs that led to the surface.

If she had been more Indian, she would have said she had a heavy heart. She turned back to the noise and celebration in the dressing room.

The boisterous team had finally broken up to finish dressing and return home to prepare for the victory banquet. All the division's teams would be there to see the Falcons officially receive the championship trophy.

Leigh, still upset from her meeting with her mom, had been quiet on the trip home. Her dad hadn't seemed to notice as he talked about the game and how good a hockey player she was. His friends met them at their house where they were joined by other neighbours who'd heard of the team's win. They sat around the living room, talking and joking.

Leigh acknowledged their congratulations, then escaped upstairs for a quick soak in a hot tub. Her muscles were starting to tighten up to the cramping stage.

She could hear music from downstairs as the festive mood continued, with more people dropping over to offer their good wishes.

After the scene with her mother, Leigh wasn't feeling very festive herself. In fact, she wasn't even excited about winning the championship. It wasn't the same now. She went into the bathroom and sat on the edge of the tub.

Making this up to her mom would be impossible. She was just reaching for the hot water tap when she remembered about recording the recital. Rats! In all the excitement, it had completely slipped her mind. Maybe she could still catch some of the broadcast and, with a little luck, Wind Dancer's performance. At least she'd be able to tell her mom she'd seen them dance.

It was pretty feeble, but she was desperate. Leigh jumped up and headed downstairs. When she reached the landing, she could hear her father and his friends discussing the game.

"Leigh's quite the hockey player. I'm betting she'll go on to play in the NHL, with the proper coaching, of course," she heard her dad say proudly.

"Yeah, there's a couple of good players on the Falcons," she heard another voice continue. "Like that Fraser boy. Man, he can handle a stick, can't he?"

Another disembodied voice joined in. "He's an Indian kid, isn't he?"

"Actually he's Métis," she heard her father say finally.

"What's that?" the first man asked.

"Half French Canadian, half Native," her father replied.

Leigh stopped in the doorway and stared at her dad. She waited for him to speak up, to finally say, "He's Métis—like me."

Instead, all he said was, "Oh, hi honey." He got up from the sofa where he'd been sitting.

She couldn't say anything. She just stared at her dad. She knew he'd never told his friends he was Métis. In fact Leigh had never heard him admit anything to anyone about their Métis history or her mom being an Indian either. Leigh had always gone along with her dad by simply remaining quiet as well.

Leigh was suddenly so furious at her father that she was shaking. Then a curious thing happened. She stopped being angry. She became very calm.

Everything became clear to her. All this time she'd

been trying to be white when she was with her dad, and Indian when she was with her mom, being careful what she said to whom so the two worlds wouldn't slam into each other. But what if they did?

What was the worst that would happen if she talked about her Indian mother to her white friends? Her real friends wouldn't care what colour her mom was, any more than Leigh cared what colour their moms were.

Leigh was proud of her mother. She was smart and pretty, and her dancing was a wonderful gift. And would her mother really have minded if Leigh had told her about the things she did with her white friends, like playing hockey? Would it be impossible for them to work things out? Somehow Leigh didn't think her mom would mind once she'd explained everything.

She was a special, one-of-a-kind blend of both her parents and Leigh suddenly wanted the whole world to know it.

"I won't be going to the banquet tonight, Dad," she said quietly.

"What? Why not? Are you sick, Leigh?" He came over and put his hands on her shoulders. He looked concerned.

"I'm not sick, Dad. In fact I've never felt better in my whole life." She took a deep breath and began, "Mom's dance group, Wind Dancer, has a recital today and I'm going to go. I was asked to perform my Fancy Dance, but I lied and told Mom I'd hurt my ankle so I could play in the game today. If I hurry I might be able to find her and apologize. It might make up a little for the way I've treated her."

Her dad looked stunned. He stared at her for a long moment, then as though he finally understood exactly what she was really trying to say, he slowly nodded at her.

"If this is what you really want, Leigh..." he said, giving her the chance to change her mind. They both knew what her decision meant. Things would never be the same for either of them. "It is, Dad. In fact it's the one thing I *do* want. I hope you understand."

He turned to his assembled friends. "It seems we have a change in the game plan, guys. I have to take my daughter to a dance recital in which her mother's native dance group is performing. I'll see you at the office on Monday."

The men looked at her father, then at each other.

"Sure, no problem, we'll see you at work," one of them said rather awkwardly.

Her father walked with them to the door.

They looked more than a little confused, Leigh thought. This should make for interesting conversation over coffee at the office.

★★★

The recital was still underway when Leigh arrived. Backstage at the auditorium, there was a buzz of activity.

There were brightly costumed dancers from lots of different cultures. Leigh saw Russian dancers wearing blousy white shirts and bright red baggy pants which would let them do the spectacular kicks they were famous for. She saw ladies in kimonos from Japan and girls in kilts representing Scotland. She stared at the ladies from Indonesia with their beautiful costumes and exaggerated makeup.

Leigh spotted her mother and the Wind Dancers through a break in the crowd of performers backstage.

She walked up to her mom and took a deep breath.

"Mom," she began, then she didn't know what to say. "I'm, I'm so sorry, about everything," she stammered. "I didn't understand a lot of things until today. I know I should have told you about my hockey, but I thought you wouldn't let me play. I love you and I'm proud of you, really, I just didn't know what to do so you and Dad wouldn't be mad…"

Her mother stared at her, then a small smile started on her face.

"It's okay, Leigh. I know it's been hard for you. I understand." She held her arms out to her daughter. "Everything's going to be fine. We're going to have to sit down and talk, all of us."

Leigh smiled up at her mom. It really was going to be all right. Everything was going to be great.

Then she thought of something. "I feel so bad. I wanted to dance tonight but I didn't know how to be in the recital without telling you about hockey and causing a huge problem."

Her mom's eyes crinkled with delight. "Well, if that's the way you feel, come with me."

She led Leigh into the big dressing room the dancers used to change into their colourful costumes. There, in the corner, with the trunks and cases belonging to Wind Dancer, was her beautiful dress.

"I had it packed with the other costumes and didn't have the heart to leave it behind. If you hurry you can change and join us. We're not scheduled to perform until the very end." She smiled at Leigh. "Anyone who can play hockey as well as you do should be able to handle a couple of dance numbers."

"You mean you saw me play today?" Leigh asked.

"After your neighbour told me about the game, I went down and watched you. You really are good, you know." She smiled at Leigh.

Leigh glowed under her mom's praise. "You think so? I really love hockey, Mom. I want to play in the NHL someday."

"As long as it doesn't interfere with your dancing, I can't see a problem with that," her mother smiled as she handed Leigh the dress and shawl.

"Oh, by the way, I've been saving something for you," she said, and went over to an intricately carved wooden box sitting on a table. She opened the box and lovingly took out a single eagle feather.

"This was your grandmother's when she danced and she gave it to me when I started dancing. Now, I give it to you," she held the feather out to Leigh.

Slowly, Leigh reached for the sacred symbol.

"Oh, Mom," was all she could say, "thank you."

She hurried to dress. Her mother helped her with her headdress, making sure the eagle feather was securely pinned so there was no chance of it slipping out and touching the ground. Leigh knew this was something to be guarded against. The eagle feather was a talisman treasured by all who knew how important it was.

Finally, her mother stepped back. "You look fantastic." She turned Leigh around, inspecting every detail. "Shall we go show the group? They'll be so pleased you're going to dance after all."

Leigh followed her mother toward the backstage area to find the rest of Wind Dancer. Through a break in the curtains, she glimpsed the flash of some Inuit dancers on stage in fur parkas with spears. With their dance, they enacted a ritual hunt where each dancer wore a carved mask symbolizing a different character or animal in the hunt. The trick lighting and smoke from dry ice made the scene look very eerie and unreal. Leigh wished she had more time to watch.

As they neared Wind Dancer, Leigh froze. Coming toward her through the crowd were Tina and Susan. What were they doing here, and what would they say when they saw her in her costume? Her heart beat faster and she felt panic bubbling up, and then that wonderful calm came over her again.

Her mother looked at her questioningly, then followed Leigh's gaze to the approaching girls.

When Tina and Susan saw Leigh, they stopped and stared.

Leigh took a deep breath. A whole new part of her life was about to begin.

"Hey, guys." She swallowed hard and smiled at her friends. "Tina, Susan, I'd like you to meet my mom. Her dance group is representing the Tsuu T'ina nation in the recital tonight." Leigh's voice was clear and filled with pride.

"Your mom's a dancer!" Tina blurted out. "When she was never around, I just naturally assumed she was in the witness protection program."

"Naturally." Leigh wondered if Tina was ever for real.

"Hi, I'm Tina, Leigh's best friend." She extended her hand. "Nice to meet you, Mrs. Aberdeen. Leigh's never told me anything about you," she glanced at her friend, "but I guess that's all going to change now."

"Starting first thing tomorrow morning when you come over for breakfast," Leigh promised. "What are you guys doing here anyway?"

"Susan came down to wish her cousin good luck with her Scottish sword dancing and I wanted to see what a TV production looked like," Tina volunteered. "But from that totally cool getup you have on, it looks like I'll be able to wish you good luck as well."

"Oh, you mean this particularly stunning outfit?" Leigh extended her arms so the girls got the full effect of the costume. "This, ladies, is a genuine Fancy Dress handmade by my mom for me to perform a genuine Fancy Dress dance."

"It's absolutely out of this world," Tina said enthusiastically.

"Yeah, it's great," Susan said quietly, not looking at Leigh.

Leigh slowly lowered her arms. Maybe she'd misjudged Susan when she'd considered her a friend.

Suddenly Susan took a step toward Leigh. There were tears in her eyes. "I can't stand it anymore. Leigh, I have something to tell you," she said, her voice wavering.

"What is it? What's the matter?" Leigh asked, alarmed by Susan's outburst.

"It's about those phone messages and nasty notes you got…"

Leigh remembered how Jimmy had denied knowing anything about them when she'd confronted him in the dressing room.

Susan went on, "I was the one who did all that stupid stuff. I was just trying to help my brother get you off the team. I didn't know you then." She looked at Leigh. "I'm so sorry. I've wanted to tell you, but I thought you'd hate me."

Leigh thought about everything that had happened. Even after hearing Susan's confession, Leigh couldn't be angry with her. She liked Susan.

"You made a mistake. We all make mistakes sometimes. The important thing is you figured it out and you tried to make it right." She smiled at Susan. "No worries."

"Hey," Tina interrupted, looking at Leigh's brightly beaded moccasins, "Does this mean you've traded in your skates for those moccasins?"

"No way. They'll do just fine sharing the same shelf." Leigh smiled up at her mom.

"Would you girls like to meet the other dancers Leigh will be performing with tonight?" her mother asked, motioning toward the beautifully costumed troupe.

"That would be wonderful," Susan nodded.

"All right!" Tina agreed enthusiastically. "Wait till I tell everyone my best friend's in show biz!"

She grabbed Susan's arm and began piloting her toward the waiting dancers.

"You have very nice friends, Leigh." Her mom put an arm around Leigh's shoulders and drew her close. "But I want you to realize not everyone will react to you like they did. Just remember—you can't help the way other people feel about you. All you can do is make sure you like the way you feel about yourself."

Leigh looked up at her mother and smiled. "From now

on I know I'm going to like myself and my life a lot more."

Her mom gave her shoulder a little squeeze.

They turned and together, Leigh and her mother walked toward the music and lights.

ACKNOWLEDGEMENTS

The author would like to thank the elders and staff at the Plains Indians Cultural Survival School; Diane Gregoire at Zone 3, Regional Council, Métis Nation of Alberta; Virginia Hager for her help with the dancing terminology; and Harley Crowchild for his helpful advice.

MORE SPORTS, MORE ACTION
www.lorimer.ca

CHECK OUT THESE OTHER HOCKEY STORIES FROM LORIMER'S SPORTS STORIES SERIES:

A Goal in Sight
By Jacqueline Guest

Aiden is the toughest defenceman in his Calgary hockey league, often spending as much time in the penalty box as on the ice—and that's the way he likes it. But when he hits another player after a game, Aiden finds himself charged with assault and sentenced to one hundred hours of community service. Unfortunately, Eric, the blind hockey player he's assigned to help, is not exactly what he had in mind...

Rink Rivals
By Jacqueline Guest

When the Selkirk family moves from their remote Cree community to Calgary, life turns upside down for twin brothers Evan and Brynley. Evan has always been the family hockey hero, while Bryn prefers the piano to the puck. But in Calgary, Bryn trades piano practice for hockey practice to impress a new girlfriend, while Evan starts running with a bad crowd and neglecting the game. As the brothers' lies get them into deeper and deeper trouble, they have to rely on each other to gain the courage to set things right.

LORIMER